OUTLAW'S FORTUNE

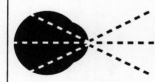

This Large Print Book carries the
Seal of Approval of N.A.V.H.

OUTLAW'S FORTUNE

W. W. Lee

Thorndike Press • Thorndike, Maine

Published in 1994 by arrangement with Walker Publishing Company, Inc.

All the characters and events portrayed in this work are fictitious.

Thorndike Large Print ® Popular Series.

The tree indicium is a trademark of Thorndike Press.

The text of this Large Print edition is unabridged.
Other aspects of the book may vary from the original edition.

Set in 16 pt. News Plantin.

Printed in the United States on acid-free, high opacity paper. ∞

Library of Congress Cataloging in Publication Data

Lee, W. W. (Wendi W.)
    Outlaw's fortune / W.W. Lee
      p.   cm.
    ISBN 0-7862-0161-4 (alk. paper : lg. print)
    1. Birch, Jefferson (Fictitious character) — Fiction.
2. Large type books. I. Title.
    [PS3562.E3663O94 1994]
    813'.54—dc20
                                     93-47267

For my dad,
Harvey A. Weberg

CHAPTER 1

Standing on the railroad platform, conductor Ned Murchison could hear the screech and groan of the train's brakes long before the Albuquerque train pulled into the station. Pueblo, Colorado, was the end of the line, and there would be a change in train personnel for the trip back to Albuquerque that afternoon. The smell of burning oil and hot iron hung heavy in the air, a scent that never completely went away, even with the strongest breeze.

But today, as most days, there had not been a breeze, and Murchison was working on the platform in his shirt-sleeves. Later he would have to put on his long, double-breasted frock coat when it was time to punch tickets on the train. Inside the cars would be hot, but for now, he could relax on the platform as the train pulled in and he directed passengers, answered questions about time-tables, and supervised the porters as they unloaded and loaded luggage. Murchison paused to scratch his muttonchops and adjust his trainman's cap when he felt a tap on his shoulder and turned around to face the stationmaster. Quint was tall and thin, and he never appeared to sweat, an ability that Murchison envied. A squat, older man with a no-nonsense demeanor accompanied Quint.

"This here is James Masters," Quint told Murchison. "He's a railroad agent and he's got something important to tell you, Ned."

Murchison looked at his pocket watch before nodding pleasantly to the railroad agent. "I've got about ten minutes before I begin supervising passengers boarding, Mr. Masters. What can I do for you?"

Masters pulled a neatly folded paper from his coat pocket and handed it to Murchison. "I want you to study this, Mr. Murchison. We've had trouble with this outlaw recently."

Murchison looked at the paper; it was a wanted poster for a man named Tom Hogan. The name was familiar. As he read the physical description — tall, gaunt, mole on the left side of the nose — he raised his eyebrows and looked up. "Say, hasn't this fellow been caught yet? He's been at this sort of thing for over ten years."

Masters winced, apparently not liking to have the obvious pointed out, especially when it reflected badly on how he did his job.

"Hogan is clever," Masters said, frowning. His eyebrows moved closer together like two large gray caterpillars. "But I say he's too damn clever for his own good, and one day it'll catch up with him."

The conductor nodded, noting to himself that it hadn't caught up with Hogan yet. He handed the poster back to Masters. "I'll keep an eye out for him," Murchison assured the agent, then thought of something odd in the poster about the outlaw's method of robbery. "But don't most train robbers derail trains these days? In that case, I wouldn't see his face until he had already stopped the train — by then it would be too late."

"Hogan isn't like most train robbers. Recently he's been posing as a passenger. Then he holds up the conductor and the engine driver, forcing them to stop the train at an appointed place. Hogan's gang is usually waiting there."

Murchison nodded his understanding. "You better show this poster to all the porters as well. One of them might recognize Hogan among the passengers boarding the train."

Masters thanked him and moved off. Checking his watch again, Murchison called out the signal to board and began helping ladies and children up the steep steps into the cars, all the while watching the men who boarded and wondering if Tom Hogan, train robber, was among them. As he offered his hand to an elderly lady wearing a black lace veil, he scanned the crowd.

"Young man," the woman interrupted his thoughts with a sharp schoolteacherlike voice, "please keep your hand steady. My legs aren't what they used to be." Murchison felt the elderly lady lurch slightly as she tried to reach the train step.

"One moment, madam," Murchison said, bending down and deftly pulling a small step stool out from just inside the train. He could see the old woman smile gratefully through the thick veil. What an ugly old woman, Murchison thought as she entered the train. He immediately chastised himself for his cruelty. She couldn't help the way she looked.

When everyone had boarded and all the luggage had been loaded onto the train, Murchison retrieved his frock coat and checked his watch a third time. The train wouldn't be pulling out of the station for another minute. As he was putting on his coat, he looked up and saw Masters walking toward him.

"I didn't see anyone who looked like Thomas Hogan come aboard," Murchison told him, shaking his head. "I don't suppose the porters or the stationmaster saw anything either."

Masters handed the wanted poster to the conductor. "No luck here. But take this with you. There'll be an agent at the other end of the line. I'm not going with you, because I've heard a rumor that Hogan might be here in town. Do you have a gun?"

Murchison patted the left side of his frock coat. "Right here in my Prince Albert. I keep it out of sight. Don't want to scare the ladies."

Masters nodded shortly. "Good man. Be careful." He turned and walked away.

The engineer blew the train's whistle loud and long to let everyone know that the train was about to pull out. Murchison hopped aboard just as the iron horse began to move.

The trip was routine. Murchison loved the sound of the engine chugging away and the feel of the clack of train tracks. It lulled many of his passengers to sleep before he could punch all the tickets. Since most fell asleep with their tickets clutched in their hands, it was rare that he had to wake anyone.

After punching tickets on the Pullman car,

Murchison made his way up the unreserved coaches. In the coach closest to the engine, he noticed the elderly lady with the veil sitting in the back of the car. There was a young dark-haired cowboy seated opposite her. He was slouched in his seat, his hat pulled forward slightly.

While the car wasn't crowded now, Murchison hoped that the passengers would make room for those who boarded at La Junta. He took the old lady's ticket and punched it. She was going only as far as Thatcher.

At La Junta, more passengers boarded. Ten miles past Timpas, Murchison walked up the cars punching new tickets. When he reached the first car, the old lady hailed him.

"Young man!"

He turned toward her and smiled. "Yes, ma'am?"

"I want to get off now," she said, sounding insistent.

"Yes, ma'am," he replied placatingly. "We're almost to Thatcher. You get off there."

"How long till we arrive?" she asked, this time in a sweet tone of voice.

From an inside pocket of his coat Murchison took out his Raymond watch and consulted it. "Less than half an hour."

"But I want to get off *now*."

Murchison looked out the window at the barren land — no farm, no fence, not even a tree. Surely her brains were addled. He had dealt with the elderly before, and knew that if he was firm but civil, he would eventually calm her down.

"Ma'am, I — " he started to say politely, turning to face her. Suddenly, he faced down the barrel of a pistol. The little old lady had taken off her hat and veil. Murchison was startled to see that her hair had come off, too, revealing a shorter shock of white hair. It took him a moment longer to realize that he was face-to-face with Tom Hogan, the train robber.

An involuntary groan escaped from Murchison as he ran down the list of physical characteristics from the wanted poster: tall, gaunt, white hair, mole on the left side of the nose. Hogan, as the elderly passenger, had walked with a stoop to hide his height.

Murchison thought about the gun in his coat pocket and wondered if he would get a chance to use it.

Hogan, his eyes fastened on the conductor and one hand occupied with the gun, was struggling out of the dress.

During his ten years with the railroad, Murchison had been robbed only twice. Of course, train robbers usually waylaid a train by derailing it.

Tom Hogan's way of robbing a train was much more clever, and less disastrous. As much as Murchison detested what was happening, he had to admire Hogan's cleverness. Murchison started to put his hands in his pockets without thinking.

"Keep your hands where I can see them," Hogan growled quietly.

Murchison noticed that the young cowboy who had been napping in the seat opposite Hogan was no longer there. No one else was facing them; so far, the robbery was taking place without anyone else being aware of it. Maybe the cowboy would return and distract Hogan. At that moment the conductor felt a presence behind him and slowly looked around. It was the young cowboy — with his gun drawn. But instead of pointing his weapon at Hogan, he was aiming for Murchison.

"That sure was some disguise," the cowboy addressed Hogan with admiration. "No one thought it would work except you."

Hogan grinned. He had thrown his disguise to the side, revealing a white cotton shirt, a brown broadcloth vest, and nankeen pants. "Sure did. Now let's get this train stopped. I'll go help the conductor uncouple the link-and-pin. You stay here and keep an eye on everyone. We'll get this train stopped in just about the right place."

Murchison and Hogan marched up the aisle, with the cowboy following behind. "Don't nobody make any sudden moves," the cowboy announced in a loud, reedy voice. "This is a robbery, and we don't want to hurt nobody. . . ."

Murchison didn't hear the rest. He had stepped outside the car at Hogan's bidding and was staring down at the link-and-pin coupling. Murchison suddenly felt ill. Men had died trying to uncouple cars while the train was in motion. He wasn't sure whether he preferred to die with a bullet in his gut or while pulling the linchpin that held the passenger cars to the cab and open tender.

"Well, what are you waiting for?" Hogan yelled over the sound of the train.

"I'm waiting for someone with enough courage to pull the pin out," Murchison yelled back. "It would be less dangerous for us to climb over the open tender into the cab and get the engine driver to apply the brakes."

"Is that what you're suggesting?" Hogan asked.

Murchison's thoughts were flying furiously. If he got Hogan to agree, maybe he could push him off the train, or knock the gun out of his hand. It occurred to him that maybe the engine driver or the stoker would see them climbing over the woodpile on the open tender and be ready for Hogan when he tried to enter the cab.

Hogan stared at Murchison for a moment, then motioned with his gun. "If you ain't gonna do it, then I'll do it. Get back inside where the kid can keep an eye on you." Murchison was about to obey when Hogan added, "And before you go, give me that weapon of yours."

Murchison sighed and opened his coat. Hogan took the pistol out of the conductor's inside coat pocket and stuck it in his own pants. "Move," he shouted.

Murchison didn't want to see Hogan die, although he was an outlaw. "You'll kill yourself if you try to pull the linchpin. I'll do it." Switching places with Hogan, he faced the coupling and grabbed the outside railing with his left hand. Murchison tried to reach the pin by bending down, but he couldn't reach far enough. Straightening up, he turned to Hogan and said, "You'll have to hold me so I don't fall under the rails. Can I trust you?"

Hogan stared at him. "I'm a train robber, not a killer. I'll hang on to you." He gripped the conductor's left wrist and Murchison edged out farther, bent down as far as he dared without losing his balance, and grasped the pin. With a quick, hard tug, the coupling came loose; the cab and open tender began to move away from the rest of the cars. Hogan pulled him in and Murchison breathed deeply for the first time, the pin still clutched in his hand and his legs a little shaky.

"You did good," Hogan said gruffly. "Let's go back inside."

Inside the car, the passengers were quiet, fearful eyes trained on the young cowboy with the gun. He was strutting back and forth, as nervous as a mountain cat staring down a rattlesnake. Murchison saw relief in the kid's eyes when Hogan took over. It's probably the boy's first train job, Murchison thought.

He wondered where the rest of the gang was, if they had already boarded. The train was still moving, but had slowed down enough for outlaws on horses to board. As if in answer to his question, the sound of hooves drumming the dry ground grew closer and stopped. He also heard the creak of wagon wheels.

"Guess everyone's here, just in time," Hogan addressed the cowboy. "The passengers and the porters in the other cars must be getting restless."

A large man with black hair stepped into the back of the car. He wore a bandanna over his face, but Murchison could tell that he had a bushy beard underneath. The backs of his arms were covered with thick black hair as well. His eyes were light blue, so light they almost looked white. Murchison felt a shiver run up his spine when the mysterious outlaw looked him over. A moment later, the outlaw dismissed the conductor and turned to Hogan. "Hey, Hogan," he said hoarsely, "the boys are taking care of the other passengers and hitting the mail car."

Hogan grimaced and said in a peeved voice, "I told you not to use my name."

The black-haired man shrugged. Murchison thought he saw him grin under the bandanna. "You think they don't know already?"

The cowboy spoke nervously. "Back at the depot, they was showing a wanted poster around, Hogan. They know about you. This conductor probably recognized you already."

Hogan gazed at the conductor for a moment.

The thought occurred to Murchison that Hogan might decide to kill everyone in the car now that he had been identified by name. Hogan had told Murchison that he wasn't a killer — he easily could have killed Murchison after he had uncoupled the cars from the engine.

Hogan broke into a grin, looking downright pleased. "So you know who I am?"

"I figured it out right after you took off the hat and wig," Murchison admitted in a mild tone.

Hogan looked satisfied. "That was a pretty good disguise, if I do say so myself." He turned to the kid. "Let's get moving. I want us out of this area in ten minutes. The engine driver will figure out that something's wrong and reverse the cab soon."

"I'm not so sure this is a good idea," the cowboy said, sounding as if he had just come to his senses. "Maybe if we leave now without the stolen goods, they won't press charges."

The black-haired man's eyes narrowed. "Tom, I told you we shouldn't have brought him with us. Let's leave him here, kill everyone in the car."

Hogan clapped his young companion on the shoulder and replied in a calm voice, "Oh, I think my young friend here is expressing some doubts, the same as most men do on their first time out. Don't you worry about him. I'll watch out for him." Hogan's voice took a nasty turn. "And I told you before, no killin'. That's the golden rule when you work with me. Now let's see to the other cars before anyone starts getting any ideas about being a hero."

It was now clear that Hogan was in charge and would not stand for any gun play. Murchison realized he had been holding his breath throughout this exchange and now he let it out, slow and shaky.

Taking the conductor with them, the three outlaws stripped all the passengers in the cars of their money and jewelry as they headed toward the back of the train. It was hard for the conductor to watch as sobbing women pleaded with the outlaws not to take their wedding bands. But everything was taken. Hogan was firm about that. He told one woman, "It'll be fine, missus. You just wait. When your husband hears what happened to you he'll go out and buy you an even nicer ring."

Once they left the passenger car, the outlaws and Murchison entered the mail car, where a gold bullion shipment was being guarded by two government agents. No doubt, this was why the outlaws had chosen to rob this train. Both guards and the brakeman had been knocked out and tied up by a couple of outlaws who had pushed their way into the mail car soon after the train was stopped. Murchison bent down to examine the guards. They were unconscious but alive, as was the brakeman.

As if Hogan knew what his captive was thinking, he said, "I told 'em not to shoot unless they had to. We don't want a murder hanging over our heads."

As far as Murchison could tell, there were about six outlaws in all. In less than ten minutes, they loaded as much of the bullion as they could onto a wagon. In the distance, the sound of a train whistle could be heard and black smoke could be seen.

"Let's get out of here," Hogan shouted to his men. They mounted their horses, two men on the wagon, and took off at a gallop. Murchison stared after them, wondering how he was going to explain to the railroad agent in Albuquerque that the train had been held up by Tom Hogan dressed as a little old woman.

CHAPTER 2

Jefferson Birch rode into Albuquerque, and the first thing he did was take care of his horse.

He tethered Cactus to a post and watched the horse drink from the water trough. Although nearly sixteen years old, Cactus was still a good, strong horse. But Birch was more careful with him these days.

Birch looked around the busy town.

The countryside of New Mexico was a lot like Birch's home state, Texas. He hadn't been back there since he quit the Rangers, sold his ranch, and paid his last respects to the graves of his wife and child. That was four years ago.

Since then, drifting had become a way of life for Birch. For the past few years he found himself traveling aimlessly out west, up to Oregon, Wyoming, Nevada, and northern California. As the winters began to take their toll on him physically, Birch was drawn to warmer climates as winter drew near, places where there wouldn't be a chill in the air by September. Southern Colorado was such a place.

Just before Birch left northern California, his ranch boss had given him a letter of introduction to take to his brother-in-law, who owned a silver-mining operation in Cripple Creek, Colorado. In September, Birch reached the mine and the rancher's brother-in-law hired him on the spot as a bodyguard.

Birch worked for the owner of the mine several months, until he received a wire from Arthur Tisdale, head of Tisdale Investigations. Birch had been employed off and on by Tisdale for several years now. The ex–Texas Ranger would drift from one ranch job to another, usually on a cattle or horse ranch, but always keeping Tisdale informed when he moved on. When Tisdale took on a client in the general area where Birch was currently located, he would send for his agent.

The work paid much better than any ranch work, generally keeping Birch fed and clothed for as long as six months at a time. This time, Tisdale's wire asked Birch to meet him in Albuquerque. Already bored guarding the owner of the large silver-mining operation, he resigned and headed for New Mexico to meet Tisdale.

Birch had been through New Mexico only once, on his way out west. Since he had never liked big cities, he avoided Albuquerque and Santa Fe that time, preferring to camp out in the desert.

Albuquerque was unlike any place he had ever been. Clusters of low, pale pueblos alternating with two-story brick buildings rose up from the dusty, barren ground. Birch felt the warmth of the sun wash over him as it had when he had lived in Texas.

He went to the first hotel he saw and asked the desk clerk whether Arthur Tisdale was staying there. Before the clerk could answer, Birch heard his boss's voice.

"Ah, there you are, Birch."

Jefferson Birch turned around to see Arthur Tisdale, a neat and tidy little man with a handlebar mustache, wearing a black woolen suit. Tisdale extended his soft, manicured hand. Birch grasped Tisdale's hand firmly and shook it.

"Good to see you again after all this time," Tisdale went on. As if to show how glad he was to see Birch, Tisdale awkwardly clapped his agent on the back.

"When are we meeting the Mr. Winslow you mentioned in your wire?" Birch asked, not one to spend much time on amenities.

"Well, as soon as you like. He told me to bring you right to his office as soon as you got in." Tisdale hesitated, then added, "Of course, if you need time to check in and clean up, or a meal, we can do that first."

Birch shook his head. He was too curious about this job. "I'm fine."

They walked outside and headed toward Cactus, who was shifting nervously from one leg to another. Tisdale raised his eyebrows and asked, "Did you take the train down?"

"No," Birch replied. "Cactus doesn't travel well on trains. He gets skittish."

"You really care about that animal, don't you?"

"He's getting a little long in the tooth . . ." Birch said with a shrug. "Cactus has been with me since I joined the Rangers." Since my wife and son died, he thought to himself. The horse is my only tie to the past. Taking up Cactus's reins, he added, "Maybe we should find a stable to board him."

"There's one on the way to the vice president's office," Tisdale replied.

After leaving Cactus munching contentedly on a bag of oats, they continued to the offices of the Santa Fe Railroad. Upon arriving at the low, whitewashed pueblo structure, the two agents were immediately ushered into Winslow's office. He had obviously been waiting for them, his railroad watch in his slack hand, his face turned toward a window that opened onto the train tracks that ran by the back of the building.

Russell Winslow, the vice president of the Santa Fe Railroad, was small in stature, but had a commanding presence. His graying blond hair was unkempt, his starched collar thrown off, as if he wore it in the morning to please his wife before he went off to work, then discarded it once he was in his office. He came around his desk to greet Birch and Tisdale and warmly shook their hands. "I'm glad you could get here so quickly," he said to Birch, his voice quite deep. "Well, gentlemen, shall we get right down to business?" He indicated the high-backed chairs that surrounded a round pine table. "This is my own version of King Arthur's Round Table. I find it more comfortable than sitting behind a desk."

While Tisdale and Birch settled at the table, Winslow went back to his desk to retrieve a paper. "I want you to look at this wanted poster." He handed it to Tisdale, who glanced at it before handing it to Birch.

Winslow continued, "Thomas Hogan is a

smart outlaw. These bills are handed out to every porter, conductor, and stationmaster. Hogan's been robbing our trains for almost ten years, and our railroad agents have been unable to catch him. We had even hired a larger agency than yours, but with no results. Regardless of what we do, Hogan manages to elude us." Winslow pounded his fist on the table surface for emphasis.

"What makes you think we can handle a job like this when your agents have failed?" Birch asked. He could feel Tisdale's cold stare. It was not good business to raise doubts in a potential client's mind.

The question didn't seem to faze Winslow. Instead, he nodded approvingly and said, "Unfortunately, most railroad agents don't have a wide range of experience. Don't get me wrong, they are all good men. And they are good at what they do. But most don't have tracking abilities or deductive powers."

Birch shifted in his seat, still studying the poster, and asked, "What about the other agency, the larger one?"

Winslow smiled, but there was no warmth in his expression. "I think you know which agency I speak of, Mr. Birch." There was an appreciative silence, then he said, "While it is a good agency, everything they do seems to generate too much publicity lately, and I don't want the newspapers alerting Hogan and this gang that we're looking for them. Your agency has the reputation of being discreet."

Tisdale broke in to ask, "What is it you want my agent to do exactly?"

"I want Hogan caught and I want him caught now, if possible, before he ruins the Santa Fe's name any further. And I think you are just the man for the job, Mr. Birch. At least, that's what I've heard from Mr. Tisdale here and several other sources."

Someone knocked at the door and stuck his head in. "Sorry to bother you, Mr. Winslow, but I need your signature on these documents. The train's going to leave in ten minutes, and I need to get the papers on the mail car immediately. Also, there's something you ought to know about." The clerk looked over at Winslow's visitors.

A flicker of impatience crossed Winslow's face, then he nodded. "If you'll excuse me, gentlemen, this will only take a moment."

When Winslow was gone, Birch turned to Tisdale and held out the wanted poster. "You'll have to do this one without me. I can't take this case."

"What?" Tisdale said, looking stricken. He took back the poster without looking at it,

28

still watching Birch's impassive face. "But why? I don't understand . . ."

Birch hesitated, looking away. "It's personal." He didn't like to be so vague, but he couldn't outright tell Tisdale that his reasons were his own and it was none of Tisdale's business. "Look," Birch amended, "you don't have to say anything to him right away — I'll stay for the rest of the meeting. But once you've found another agent, you can tell Mr. Winslow that someone else has taken over the case."

"But none of my other agents are even close to this area," Tisdale pointed out, "and Winslow has even said he's satisfied with you." When Birch remained silent, Tisdale looked exasperated. "It could take up to ten days to get someone in on this case. Please reconsider, Birch."

Birch shook his head briefly and looked straight at Tisdale. "I'm sorry. It's personal," he repeated.

Winslow came back into the office, looking agitated. His face had turned bright red and his pale hair looked even more untidy than when Tisdale and Birch first met him. "I just received word that Tom Hogan has held up another train. Robbed the passengers and got away with a shipment of gold bullion."

"How did he do it? Did he sabotage the

tracks?" Tisdale asked.

Winslow shook his head, momentarily at a loss for words. In a low voice, he said, "He dressed up like a little old lady."

"He what?" Birch asked, leaning forward as if he couldn't believe what he was hearing.

"I said, he was disguised as a little old lady passenger." Winslow stood up and started pacing. He ran his hand through his hair and sighed. "Apparently he had an accomplice with him, a young cowboy no one's ever seen before. The rest of his gang was waiting along the tracks. Hogan had the conductor uncouple the link-and-pin. The engine kept going. The mail car and the passenger cars were left stranded."

There was an uncomfortable silence. Abruptly Winslow told Tisdale and Birch, "Gentlemen, I want this man stopped. Find the gold if you can, but I want Hogan . . . dead or alive!"

"Dead or alive?" Birch spoke up. "Has he ever killed anyone?"

"No, at least not during any robberies of our trains. But I want to make an example out of him."

Tisdale stood up. "I believe we can help you. I will get right on the case."

Birch rose, shook hands with Winslow and

asked him, "Does your conductor have any idea which way the gang might have gone?"

Tisdale gave Birch a quizzical look.

Winslow shook his head. "I don't know. But you're welcome to ask him. My personal assistant, Mr. Daniels, can direct you to the conductor. Thank you and good afternoon, gentlemen."

Thus dismissed, Birch and Tisdale went into the outer office. Daniels, a thin man with solemn features, sat behind a polished oak desk, his shirt-sleeves pushed up, an accounting book in front of him. He looked up from sharpening his pencil with a small penknife. "Is the meeting over?" he asked, setting his pencil and penknife aside and standing up.

"Yes, it is," Tisdale replied in a bewildered voice. He was still watching Birch out of the corner of his eye. Then he turned his attention to Daniels and said, "I believe we'd like to question the conductor."

Daniels came around his desk. "If you'll follow me, gentlemen."

CHAPTER 3

Daniels led Jefferson Birch and Arthur Tisdale out of the building and over to the depot. They entered the back room inside the depot, a large dim room with several tables and chairs. A large lantern hung in the middle, suspended from the ceiling, and gave off kerosene fumes.

There were three men in the room. One man looked up when they entered, and Birch thought he looked like the stationmaster. Daniels ignored the man and turned to a solidly built man with iron-gray hair and muttonchops. He wore the Prince Albert frock coat that distinguished conductors from the rest of the train crew. His trainman's hat rested on the table along with some tickets and a schedule. He had just started to wind his watch when Daniels approached.

"This is Ned Murchison, the conductor on the train that was robbed," Daniels told them, then explained to Murchison that Birch and Tisdale wanted an account of what had happened.

Birch glanced at the tickets and a marked schedule on the table next to Murchison. He had apparently been counting tickets before they came in. Now, he put his business aside and his watch back in his pocket.

"When did the robbery take place?" Birch asked.

"This afternoon," Murchison replied. "We started out in Pueblo, Colorado, which is the northern end of the Santa Fe line right now. A railroad agent showed me the wanted poster of Hogan and told me to keep a lookout for him. He had reason to believe Hogan was in the area and was planning to rob one of our trains."

Murchison paused to wipe his brow with a handkerchief. "Well, I never saw him, though I looked around like the agent asked me to. None of the other workers saw Hogan either. Pretty soon, most of the passengers were boarded except for this little old lady who had a lot of trouble getting on the train. So I helped her.

"We started on time and had no problems until we left Timpas. Between Timpas and Thatcher, this little old lady said she wanted to get off the train."

Murchison stopped to mop his brow again.

Birch prompted him. "There was no stop between Timpas and Thatcher?"

The conductor continued. "No. The train was going at top speed when she told me. I thought she was just a bit confused."

"When did you know it was Hogan?" Tisdale asked.

"I'll never forget the sight of that sweet little old lady pullin' a gun on me," Murchison recalled pensively, "then takin' off her wig."

"I understand that Hogan made you separate the passenger cars from the engine," Birch said.

Murchison nodded and recounted what had happened.

Tisdale raised his eyebrows. "He was willing to take the chance himself?"

There was a low rumble in Murchison's throat as he cleared it. "Yeah. Well, then I decided I didn't want no greenhorn gettin' himself killed, even if he was an outlaw. Hogan held on to my arm while I uncoupled the link-and-pin."

The conductor went on to explain what happened after they went back inside the passenger car. When he had told them that the gang found the gold bullion in the mail car, Birch interrupted. "How did they carry away the bullion?"

"They had a wagon all ready for it, so they probably knew the gold was on the train."

Tisdale turned to Winslow's assistant, who until now had been silent. "Is there any way these outlaws could have known there was gold on that train?"

Daniels shrugged. "The government is secretive about the shipments. They probably loaded the gold up in the dead of night."

"I bet they stationed guards around the mail car all night, who then stayed with the gold on the journey to Albuquerque," Birch suggested.

Daniels nodded, a wry smile twisting his features. "That's usually the procedure."

Tisdale made a noise as if he had just made the connection. "I see. So the guards were a signal to Hogan that something valuable was aboard the train."

Birch nodded in Tisdale's direction, then asked the conductor, "Would you recognize any of the other robbers?"

"There was a young man who boarded the train in Pueblo. Pretended to be a regular passenger until Hogan made his move."

"Can you describe him?"

"He was very young, probably no more than seventeen years old. He had delicate features — a thin nose and a high brow.

His hair was dark brown and shaggy, hanging down almost to his shoulders."

"What about the rest of the gang?" Birch asked. "Does anyone have a description of the others? How many were there?"

"There were six in all, I think. Three of them moved around a lot among the passengers. I asked the guards if they remembered how many outlaws came into the mail car before I got there. They thought there were three or four. From what I saw," Murchison said, "they all wore bandannas over their faces, with the exception of Hogan and his young companion."

"Did you notice anything special about any of the other outlaws?" Tisdale asked.

The conductor thought awhile. "I know one of them didn't seem to take Hogan's orders real well."

Birch nodded. "The pattern with Tom Hogan is that he hooks up with an established outlaw gang for one train robbery, then they go their separate ways. The man you described was probably the leader of the gang." Birch persisted. "You may not have seen his face, but can you tell me about his clothes, maybe his shirt, how big he was?"

Murchison frowned, stroking his muttonchops in a thoughtful manner, then replied,

"He was a big man, burly and dark. He had hairy arms, blue eyes, black hair, and although I didn't see it, I'm pretty sure he had a beard."

"How tall was he?" Birch prompted.

"Taller than me, and I'm five feet, eleven inches. I'd say a little over six feet."

"Can you think of anything else that might be helpful?"

The conductor was silent for a short time, then finally gave up. "There was such a commotion in there. The passengers were frightened and I was doing my best to ease their fears. At the same time, I was trying to learn as much as I could about the train robbers." He shook his head, looking perplexed. "That's all I can remember. But can you tell me why Hogan doesn't have a regular gang? I don't understand that."

"He probably doesn't want to be associated with any one group for too long," Birch replied. "He knows there would be a better chance of getting caught. Also, he's a loner." Birch was aware that Tisdale was looking at him in a curious manner. He ignored his employer and continued to question the conductor. "How did you get back here?"

"After the outlaws left, our cars were sitting out in the middle of nowhere. The engine driver and stoker hadn't noticed that anything was different at first. Later, the engine driver told me that he felt the engine speeding up all of a sudden. At first he thought it was because the wood was burning at a good rate and they were on a decline. But then the stoker got suspicious and climbed out of the engine and onto the open tender. When he noticed that the rest of the train wasn't there, he called to the engine driver to set the brakes. By the time they got the train in reverse, the outlaws were gone."

Tisdale pointed out, "There wasn't much they could have done anyway."

"Short of getting shot for their trouble," Murchison agreed.

"If you recall anything else," Birch told Murchison, "contact Mr. Tisdale here." He thanked the conductor for his cooperation.

"I tell you, I don't think I'll ever forget that day," Murchison replied before going back to his work. "Even when I'm retired, I'll still be telling this to my grandchildren."

Daniels led Birch and Tisdale away. "What else do you need?" he asked solicitously.

"Do you have a passenger list?" Birch asked. "Maybe we can interview a few of the people who made Albuquerque their final stop."

Daniels nodded and made a notation on

the pad that he carried. "Mr. Murchison wrote down everyone's name and address after the robbery. I'll get the list for you."

Tisdale gave him the name of his hotel, then the assistant left.

"You seem to know a lot about Tom Hogan," Tisdale said to a grim-faced Birch. "Am I to assume that you've changed your mind about this case?"

Birch grimaced. "Winslow didn't leave me much choice."

"Why do you say that?" Tisdale asked, cocking his head to one side.

"Another man might get trigger-happy and kill Hogan just to make his job easier." Birch sighed, rubbed the back of his neck, and added, "Maybe Winslow did me a favor. I should have confronted Hogan a long time ago." With a sober expression, he looked into the distance.

Tisdale frowned but didn't ask about Birch's cryptic remark. "Well, then," he said, "I suppose there's not much more to do on this case until we get the passenger list."

Birch didn't agree. "We can pay a visit to the sheriff's office and look over the current wanted posters. The conductor gave us a partial description of one of the outlaws, probably the leader."

"Good idea," Tisdale said enthusiastically.

"It's plain to see why you're my best investigator."

Birch suppressed a smile as they started out for the sheriff's office.

"We're lucky that Murchison had the sense to write down passenger names after what he'd just been through," Tisdale noted. "He's a brave man."

"Observant, too."

The sheriff's office was in a low, white pueblo building with bars on the windows. The heat shimmered off the ground and the buildings, giving everything the illusion of a wavy reflection in a mirror. Once they stepped inside the office and closed the door, the dark, enclosed space felt considerably cooler for the first few minutes.

A tall, spare man with coarse dark hair and olive skin greeted them.

Looking around the room, Birch thought the furnishings were as spare as the man himself. A desk and two chairs were all that could be found. There was not even a hat rack. Instead, there was a row of thick pegs extending from one wall as if they had grown there. The sheriff's hat hung on one; the rest were empty.

"You must be Arthur Tisdale and his agent," the man said. He must have seen the surprise on Tisdale's face, because he

40

explained, "Russell Winslow told me that you would be stopping by. My name is Ray Gutierrez." Sheriff Gutierrez shook hands with Tisdale, then with Birch who introduced himself.

"You boys just come in here to pay your respects to the law, or do you need something?" Gutierrez asked.

Birch spoke up. "I'd like to see your posters."

The sheriff nodded, narrowing his eyes. "You want to see if you can match up some of the accomplices."

Birch was impressed.

Gutierrez pointed to a pile of papers that was sitting on a small table in the corner of the office. "I'm afraid they're not organized. And some of these men are either dead or behind bars by now. I haven't had much time to go over them lately."

Birch shuffled through the posters. "Maybe we can help you. If we see anyone here that we know is dead or in jail, we'll pull the poster." He handed a stack to Tisdale.

Tisdale looked blankly at the posters. "Who are we looking for?" he asked.

Birch said patiently, "We're looking for a gang of four or five outlaws. Since that one young cowboy didn't wear a bandanna, he must be a new face. So look for a gang of four whose leader has black hair, a beard, and hairy arms and is six feet tall with a burly build."

Tisdale nodded, a look of relief on his face. They spent the next hour carefully reading the posters. Sheriff Gutierrez also supplied newspaper articles with descriptions of local outlaws and the crimes they recently committed, then he excused himself to handle some business outside the office.

When they were done, there was a small stack of posters describing outlaws who were dead or had been apprehended. Both Tisdale and Birch had larger piles of rejected posters. Birch had two posters reserved. Tisdale had one before him.

"Let's see what you have," Tisdale said, motioning to Birch to come over to him. Birch was irritated for a moment. He felt that Tisdale was trying to horn in on his investigation, but it would do him no good to argue or become difficult now. From past experience, he knew Tisdale had to feel as though he was in control. Birch got up from his chair and moved closer to Tisdale.

Tisdale took Birch's posters and studied them. "The George Timmons gang and Kane Dunmore." He fell silent again as he looked over the two posters. Then he nodded. "Nice work. It could be either. They both fit the

42

description. Which one do you favor?"

Birch tapped the poster in Tisdale's right hand. "Kane Dunmore. He's been seen more often in the Colorado area. Timmons lives farther out near the Arizona border. What about your poster?"

Tisdale shook his head and handed it to Birch. "This one was the closest I could find. But none of these men fits the conductor's description as perfectly as Kane Dunmore." He pointed to the description on his poster. "See, the leader of this gang fits the general physical description, but there are only three outlaws in the gang."

Birch nodded and set the papers down on the desk between them. "How long are you staying here?"

Tisdale frowned. "I thought I'd head back tomorrow, but I can stay longer if you need me." The head of Tisdale Investigations paused, apparently having a question of his own that he didn't know how to ask.

Birch felt a small growing dread form in the pit of his stomach.

"Why did you take the case, Birch?"

Birch leaned back, avoiding Tisdale's frank expression. "Same reason I didn't want to take it in the first place . . . it's personal."

Tisdale persisted. "You know whether Hogan's still riding with that gang?"

43

Birch shook his head. "No, he's not. In the past, he's always split up the money, then gone his own way. I have no reason to think he would do anything different this time."

"Then why are we both sitting here looking for the gang? Shouldn't you be riding after Hogan? I can organize a posse to go after the gang."

Birch suppressed a grim smile. "I don't have to ride after Hogan. I have an idea where he's going. He's heading south to the border."

Tisdale sat up. "He'll have to pass through Albuquerque. Maybe we should join forces with Gutierrez and start looking for him here."

Birch shook his head. "He won't pass through here. Since he robbed a train up north, I'm pretty sure he's heading south. But he'll probably avoid a big city like Albuquerque. I'll leave town by tomorrow and catch up to him."

"Do you think you can find Hogan before he pulls another train robbery?"

Birch got up and stretched, his chair squeaking in relief. "I think . . . I haven't had anything to eat since morning. Let's go find a nice steak somewhere."

Sighing in frustration, Tisdale got up. "Okay, but answer me this: Do you want

44

me to stay on here for a few more days?"

Birch nodded. "I should probably leave tomorrow. Someone will have to interview those witnesses. One of those passengers may remember more details to bear out Murchison's description. And someone may have seen something that they don't realize is important. I think we can safely bet that Kane Dunmore's gang robbed that train with Hogan, but I want to be sure. You can stay here and wire the law in Colorado, maybe find out if the Dunmores show their faces around somewhere."

"All right. I'll stay," Tisdale agreed. "What should I do if none of the passengers has anything more to add?"

"Either way, contact the authorities up in Pueblo and give them the information you have. They can start looking for Dunmore."

As Birch started for the door, Tisdale cleared his throat. Turning around, Birch grinned and took his hat from Tisdale's extended hand.

"Thanks," he said, jamming his hat on his head.

CHAPTER 4

That evening, with nothing more to do until morning, Tisdale strolled along the main street and took in the sights and sounds of Albuquerque while he waited for Birch to check into the hotel. The town was an exotic mixture of cultures to him: Rough-and-ready saloons and gambling parlors stood next to cantinas where the scent of spicy food cooking wafted through the doors. He watched women walk by wearing loose, colorfully embroidered white cotton blouses, red or blue skirts, and carrying baskets of tortillas and chilies balanced on their heads and hips. Some of them eyed him with sly smiles on their faces as they passed by. Astounded by this boldness, Tisdale could feel the heat of embarrassment — or was it excitement — warm his face.

He met Birch coming out of the hotel and fell into step beside him. "Have you ever been here before?" he asked.

"A few times," Birch admitted, "when I was with the Rangers."

"Then maybe you know where we can get a good meal," Tisdale replied.

Birch drew his eyebrows together in thought. "Well, it depends on if you want that steak we talked about earlier. You ever had Mexican food?"

"No, I haven't." The truth was that Tisdale stuck to meat and potatoes. That's what his mother had put on the table when he was growing up, that's what he was given in the cavalry, and that's what he ate when at home in San Francisco.

Birch turned a corner, taking them off the boulevard onto a narrow side street. A few yards down, they stopped at a cantina, Birch ducking his head to enter through the small door. Once inside, Birch claimed a table for them and Tisdale quickly adjusted to the warm atmosphere, taking his jacket off and hanging it on the back of his chair. There didn't appear to be anyone there at first, but as his eyes grew used to the dark interior, a plump, middle-aged Mexican woman came forward to greet them. She wore large metal hoop earrings that swung gaily from her earlobes.

"Welcome to our humble cantina," she said, then leaned forward to peer at Birch.

"Oh, Ranger Birch! I did not recognize you at first."

"How are you, Nina?" Birch replied, smiling and taking her hands. "I'm not a Ranger anymore."

"Is that why you stopped coming here?" she asked, frowning.

"I've been away these past few years. California, Oregon, other places." Birch turned and introduced Tisdale to Nina.

"It is a pleasure to meet Mr. Birch's friends." She smiled, pumping and squeezing his hand. Tisdale wasn't sure what to do. He had never had a strange woman treat him like a long-lost relative before, so he just smiled and kept his hand as limp as a wet rag in Nina's strong grip.

"What are you cooking today, Nina?" Birch asked.

She beamed. "For you, Mr. Birch, and your friend, I will cook chicken mole." In an aside to Tisdale, Nina added, "It's his favorite dish." She hurried away. Just as they settled at the table, she came back with a bottle of tequila, a covered plate of warm tortillas, and a chunky tomato relish Birch called salsa.

As they made short work of the tortillas, salsa, and tequila, Tisdale leaned over and in a dry tone said, "You said you've only been to Albuquerque a few times?"

Birch chuckled. "With other Texas Rangers. We would meet the Arizona Rangers here to exchange prisoners or information. I guess it was more than a few times."

"I should say," Tisdale replied, then he changed the subject. "Before this assignment, you were working at a silver-mining operation, weren't you?"

Birch nodded. "I was a bodyguard for the owner. He thought everyone was out to kill him so they could take his mine away. Of course, whenever the silver was loaded on a wagon and transported to the nearest town, my employer had to fend for himself while I rode shotgun. Your wire came at the right time."

"Oh?"

"I was ready to turn in my resignation and move on."

"You seem to be drifting back toward Texas," Tisdale pointed out, taking up another tortilla and spooning salsa onto it.

Birch shrugged. "The cold weather was getting to be too much for me. And I didn't like the damp weather in California either. I wanted a mild winter, and Southern Colorado was where I ended up."

"Do you ever think you'll go back to Texas?"

Birch was quiet for a moment. "I will be going back there on this assignment."

Their main meal arrived, steaming plates of chicken covered with a dark sauce that smelled suspiciously like the hot chocolate Tisdale favored on a bitter-cold night in San Francisco. Tisdale inhaled the fragrance, then took a tentative bite. The flavor was a bit of a shock at first, not sweet as he had expected, but he soon became used to it.

In between bites of chicken mole, Tisdale talked about the cases he had assigned to other part-time agents during the last few months — who he was satisfied with, who needed to be replaced. By the time he had finished the mole, Tisdale realized how much he wanted a second helping. He stared mournfully at his empty plate before Nina came to take it away and replace it with a caramel custard that he learned was called flan, and a dark, aromatic coffee.

As they walked slowly back to the hotel, Tisdale said, "It seems to me that you and Hogan have tangled in the past. Am I correct?"

There was a small silence before a clearly uncomfortable Birch said, "We haven't tangled, exactly. How I know Tom Hogan has nothing to do with this case."

Tisdale knew he shouldn't press it, but

he couldn't help himself. "Then why did you not want to take this case? It's just not like you, Birch."

"At first, it just didn't seem like a good idea," Birch replied in a vague tone. "I'm not denying that I used to know Hogan, but I didn't think I should be the one who tracked him down at first."

"It was after Winslow put the price on his head, dead or alive, that you relented, right?" Tisdale knew he was treading a fine line here, and he expected Birch to shut down at any moment. But to his surprise, Birch answered him.

"Yes," Birch replied. "After that, it seemed I was the only one who should go after Hogan. I don't want some two-bit bounty hunter shooting Hogan's fool head off just to make it easier to bring him back to Albuquerque. Hogan may be a train robber, but he's no killer. And he doesn't deserve to die that way just to satisfy some pompous chowderhead."

Tisdale hadn't thought of Winslow as pompous, but he could understand Birch's anger. On a whim, Winslow had decided Hogan's fate as an example to other train robbers. Tisdale didn't pursue the subject of Hogan any further, and they fell into a comfortable silence until bidding each other good night at the hotel.

The next morning, Tisdale watched his agent check his gear one last time. The day was not much different from the day before: sunny, hot, and dusty.

"I think I have just about all I'll need," Birch said, turning to Tisdale. "Think you can handle it here alone?"

"Of course I can," Tisdale replied, hoping he didn't sound too sharp. He was having second thoughts about sending Birch out looking for Tom Hogan.

In the past, Birch had always been reliable and honorable. Whenever Birch kept facts to himself, Tisdale later had to admit that it had been with good reason. But Tisdale didn't get that feeling with this assignment.

"Birch, I'd like to discuss Hogan one more time," Tisdale said.

Birch already had his left boot in the stirrup and was getting ready to mount and ride. He paused, untangled his foot, and faced Tisdale. He moved over to the hitching post and leaned casually against it.

Tisdale hurried on. "I'm still a bit uneasy about handing this case to you. There's something personal about it for you, and I don't want to lose my best agent because you made a bad decision based on something that happened years ago."

Birch had tipped his hat over his forehead so Tisdale couldn't see his eyes. His jeans were already covered with the fine, white dust that was constantly moving in the warm breeze. Tisdale knew that his own black suit was beginning to look gray.

"It's true that I have something against Hogan, but it's not what you think. I give you my word that I won't let my own experience with him influence my job." Birch tipped his hat back and squinted at Tisdale in the bright sun. "But I won't tell you how I know Hogan. You'll just have to trust me."

Reluctantly, Tisdale nodded, then sighed. "I always have, haven't I?"

Birch swung up into the saddle. "I'll contact you when I reach the next town. If you have any information, wire me. Otherwise, I'll assume you have no news."

With a tip of his hat to a lady passing in front of him, Birch wheeled Cactus around and rode off.

Tisdale watched the tall, lean figure so at home in the saddle. He didn't have a good feeling about Birch on this assignment. He wished he had been able to go along to keep closer track of his agent this time.

CHAPTER 5

Floyd Coombes hated to sit in the back of a wagon on a bumpy ride, but Kane and Jasper Dunmore were the leaders. Actually, Kane was the leader and Jasper was just a bully. Floyd's back began to ache from sitting against the jarring buckboard. He knew he would have bruises there by tomorrow, but he was just happy to be free from the ropes. He still couldn't believe that an old man like Hogan had tricked all of them last night. He remembered waking up, stiff and sore, unable to move his arms or legs. It had taken him a full minute to realize that he had been drugged the night before, and was hogtied on the soft, sandy ground.

"Frank?" he had called out.

"Frank's not awake yet," a groggy voice answered. He recognized it as Kane's voice.

"Are you tied up, too?" Floyd asked.

"What do you think?" came the impatient answer. "Of course I am! That damn Hogan and his friend drugged us, tied us up, and took all the gold. They're probably a hundred miles away, if they kept driving all night."

For the first time since he'd ridden with Kane, Floyd felt helpless. Fear began to crawl up his back as he realized they might not get loose.

He voiced his fear. "So, is there a way out of this?"

There was a moment of silence, punctuated occasionally by grunting, as if Kane was trying to move around with his hands and feet tied together behind his back. "Wait a minute," he finally said. "I think he left us a knife to cut the ropes."

Floyd waited patiently for what seemed like an hour. Looking back on it, it had probably been only a few minutes.

"Damn, these ropes is cutting into my wrists," he complained, shifting from his right side to his left. He wanted to be able to see Kane. He tried to move his bound wrists behind his back, but his arms were numb. "Can you hurry it up, Kane?"

"I'm sawing the ropes as fast as I can, Floyd," Kane Dunmore snarled. "It's a little hard to do when you're trussed up like a newborn calf."

Floyd turned over in time to see Kane

drop the knife and let loose with a string of curses. "A little more toward me," Floyd called out, trying to direct Kane's clumsy effort to blindly feel around for the knife. "Are the others awake yet?"

Kane finally got a grasp on the knife and carefully positioned it until the blade was cutting the ropes again. He didn't have to answer Floyd's question, because someone else groaned.

"What happened?" Jasper asked weakly. "My head feels like I drank all the liquor in a San Francisco saloon." Floyd twisted his neck to see Jasper's narrow face and sharp chin. He had the smallest eyes Floyd had ever seen, dark brown and close-set.

"We were robbed," Kane snapped. The rope finally gave way and Kane Dunmore sat up, rubbing his rope-burned wrists. "That old geezer and that young kid tricked us. While we watched Hogan last night, that kid must have slipped something in our liquor."

Jasper grumbled. "I remember they didn't drink any, but didn't think anything of it at the time. What are we gonna do now, Kane?"

"Get these damn ropes off of everyone." Kane cut through the ropes at his ankles, then slowly stood up. He was a big, burly man with black hair and beard that gave him a fierce, warlike appearance.

Kane and Jasper were cousins of Floyd and Frank Coombes. Floyd had been a little afraid of Kane for as long as he could remember. Kane had always treated his younger cousins fairly, and when their parents died, had looked after them. But Floyd had always felt nervous around his older cousin. What scared him the most was Kane's eyes. They were a light blue, almost like blue glass. Floyd sometimes thought that if he stared into Kane's eyes long enough, he would be able to see in them all the hate and rage built up over the years.

Kane and Jasper had not had an ideal life, nor had the Coombes twins. Maybe that was why Kane insisted that his cousins come live with him and Jasper when their folks died.

Kane went over to Jasper and cut his ropes.

"Hey, Kane, over here," Frank croaked.

Kane gave the knife to Jasper. "I gotta scout around, see if they left us anything."

"Jasper," Frank said in a pleading tone.

"Just hold your horses, Francis," Jasper replied. He always called Frank by his given name, because he knew it made Frank mad. Frank didn't like the life of an outlaw and

Jasper, being a bully who considered Frank weak, couldn't resist taunting him. "I gotta free your brother. He woke up before you did."

In a few minutes, Floyd and Frank were face-to-face, mirror images of each other. The only way people could tell them apart was if they looked for the small white scar over Frank's right eyebrow, a souvenir that Jasper had given him five years ago. With curly copper hair and blue-green eyes, Floyd and Frank Coombes looked more like choirboys than hardened outlaws. They were both starting to grow beards. Floyd thought it made them look older.

"Damn, I can't believe we let Hogan slip a sleeping powder in our whiskey," Frank said. "How long do you figure we've been out?"

"Probably just overnight," Floyd replied. "I wonder how far we are from a town or a ranch."

"I'd say at least a day's walk," Kane said. He had found a bag dangling from a tree near their site. "We have just about enough food for one day if we don't get greedy."

"What're we gonna do, Kane?" Frank asked. Floyd winced at the plaintive tone of Frank's question. Frank had always been the dreamer, the romantic. He had oftentimes told Floyd that he wanted to go to San Francisco or New Orleans and become a big-time gambler. But Floyd had seen how unlucky Frank was with cards. He wasn't much better at robbing stagecoaches, either. He hated to see women cry when they had to give up their jewelry.

Floyd had always been considered the rash, headstrong twin, but he wouldn't have chosen to become an outlaw either. He just didn't mind it as much as Frank did. Floyd wasn't sure what he would have wanted to do, but it wouldn't have been robbing stagecoaches for a living. He hated going into hiding, running from the law, and becoming suspicious of every stranger who passed by. He couldn't shoot a gun all that well, either.

On the other hand, Kane and Jasper seemed to have been born outlaws. They rode well, shot well, and robbed well. It was as if this was their calling. They were also the meanest sons of bitches Floyd had ever known. If they hadn't been related to Floyd and Frank, they probably wouldn't have taken them into the gang.

"We're going to find the nearest town and get us some horses and guns," Kane replied. "Then we're going after the old man."

"What about his friend?" Jasper asked.

"Him too. We're going to find that gold and kill them both for making fools of us," Kane said, narrowing his eyes.

"Even if we get to a town, we don't have any money or gold to pay for horses and gear," Floyd pointed out.

Jasper gave Floyd a hard stare, then punched him in the ribs. Floyd was sure Jasper meant it as a joke, but Jasper had never known his own strength. Floyd tried not to double over in pain, pasting a brave grin on his face as if he barely noticed the jab.

"We ain't no bankers, Floyd," Jasper said sarcastically, "we're outlaws. We take what we want."

Kane gave his brother a nod of approval and a grin. "Let's go in the direction of the wagon tracks." As they started walking southeast along the Rio Grande, Kane doled out a piece of hardtack and jerky to each man. The band fell silent as they concentrated on walking and eating.

After a while, Frank spoke up again, timidly this time. "Sorry to ask this, Kane, but since we don't have no guns, how we gonna hold up a bank or a store?"

Kane silently held up the knife. Before Floyd could ask how they could hold up a bank with a knife, Kane was pointing to a moving spot in the distance. As the spot grew nearer, Floyd could see that it was a man in a small wagon, drawn by two horses.

"We got our transportation, boys." He handed the food bag to Frank without looking, then started waving his arms to attract the driver's attention.

A few minutes later, the stranger pulled back the reins and called out, "Whoa!" to his horses. The man wore a dark-blue suit that looked almost new. His coat lay neatly draped over the seat beside him, his white shirt well starched with the sleeves rolled up to his elbows. A black bag sat at his feet. Floyd figured that he must be a doctor of some sort.

"You fellas look like you ran into trouble," the driver said.

Floyd hadn't taken time to look closely at the other three — until now. They were a scruffy lot; their clothes were torn and dusty from lying on the ground for hours. The day's growth of whiskers didn't help either. Frank and I could pass as two men down on their luck, Floyd thought, but Jasper and Kane both naturally look like they want to kill someone. If he had been that fellow in the wagon, he would have grabbed a rifle just in case.

The stranger reached into a pocket in his suitcoat and drew out a pair of bifocals. That explained it, Floyd thought, the man was nearsighted.

"You need a ride into town?" the driver asked. Floyd watched as uncertainty crossed the man's face now that he could see the four men better.

Kane stepped forward, the knife grasped in his right hand, out of sight of the man in the wagon. "Yeah, mister, we need a ride."

Jasper swiftly climbed onto the wagon seat and took the reins from the driver, whose face now betrayed fear.

Floyd was jarred back to the present when the wagon went over a particularly nasty bump. He shuddered at the thought of Kane's last deed, the blood on his hands as Kane pulled the man out of his seat and took the reins.

Floyd ran a nervous hand through his hair and looked over at his brother, who was staring off into space, perhaps thinking the same thoughts. Shifting in the wagon again, Floyd wished that there was a sack of cornmeal to lean up against. He was glad that he hadn't been the man who had stopped for four strangers. He was glad his eyes weren't locked on the blade of a knife held by Kane Dunmore. He was glad he wasn't the one who wouldn't be home tonight for dinner.

CHAPTER 6

Birch followed the Rio Grande south to Belen. He found the telegraph office there, which also served as the ticket office for the railroad, and sent a wire to Tisdale. When he got no reply by the next day, he moved on. The land stretched before him, ever-changing in scenery and colors. Southeast of Albuquerque, Birch and Cactus traveled through high and low cedar-colored mesas. Dusty gray-green sagebrush dotted the landscape wherever the hardy plant could find a tenuous hold. The Rio Grande wound its sinuous way south, unconcerned by the fact that it looked out of place in the desert.

By the time Birch reached the tiny town of Joaca, the mountains had begun to edge closer to the river. He considered entering Joaca and asking around about Thomas Hogan, but decided against it. The chances of finding someone who remembered a stranger passing through were pretty slim.

Besides, Birch was sure he knew where Hogan was going, and that was where he would face the train robber.

Birch skirted Joaca and forded the river in a shallow, narrow place, taking care to look out for water moccasins that might make Cactus skittish.

At Socorro, Birch sent another wire to Tisdale, then took a hotel room for the night. Socorro was four times larger than Joaca, although that wasn't saying much. He took his evening meal at the saloon next door to his boardinghouse, and struck up a conversation with the bartender. Out of idle curiosity, and the possibility that Hogan might be in Socorro, Birch felt it was his duty to ask around for him.

"Gaunt, you say? White hair, mole on the left side of his nose," the bartender mused. He polished a shot glass until it gleamed. Birch wryly wondered how long it would remain that way. From what the bartender had been telling him, the winds came down from the mountains in the morning and laid a fine coat of grime over everything. Dust seemed to be everywhere in Socorro. "If I did see someone like that, I don't remember customers too good these days. The only thing I ever remember about a customer is the kind of coin he lays on the bar."

Birch pulled out two bits and laid it in front of the bartender.

After a moment's hesitation, the bartender said, "I think I seen someone like that a few days ago. He didn't stop overnight or nothin'. Just came in for a couple of shots of rye while his horse was being fed and watered." The bartender's face brightened as the thought settled in like Socorro dust. "Yeah, now I remember. A real generous fellow — he tipped me four bits."

"Do you happen to remember which way he was headed?" Birch asked. He laid down another two bits.

The bartender's eyes were fixed on the coins on the bar surface and he licked his dry lips.

"South, down the Rio," the bartender finally replied. He swept the coins off the counter and into his apron, then looked up at Birch, curiosity in his eyes. "He done something, maybe murdered someone? Is that why you're looking for him?"

Birch smiled. "For me to answer that, you're going to have to pay me." He drank the shot of whiskey before him, tipped his hat, and left.

By morning Birch hadn't gotten a reply to his wire, so he rode out of town. At least the bartender had confirmed that Hogan had not deviated from the route. Birch had guessed that Hogan would follow the river south to avoid the mountains.

The flat land gave way to hilly terrain again, black mountains encroaching on the banks of the Rio. Birch crossed the river again at a shallow place when he saw the land was still flat on the other side. He stopped Cactus and let the horse drink as he stared across the river to where he had just been. Scruffy ponderosa pine clung to the sides of faded sand-colored cliffs. Nothing else could live there, not even sagebrush. A piercing cry caused Birch to look up. A golden eagle circled with a small, struggling animal caught in its talons.

Looking downstream, Birch knew he was in for a few more days of rough travel. He recognized the land before him as the *Jornada del Muerto*, or Dead Man's Route. The towns would be fewer and farther between, and after passing through Valverde, there would be nothing for close to a hundred miles.

In Valverde, Birch wired Tisdale, then stayed the night in a boardinghouse next to the stable where Cactus was installed. Valverde, located about a mile from the Rio Grande, was almost as big as Socorro, but livelier. Seated at the foot of some low, unnamed mountains, the town had a variety of people, from loggers to miners to home-steaders. The Santa Fe ran through here as it had run through most of the towns along the Rio Grande.

Birch wondered if he should have taken the train, but that would have created more problems than it would have solved. He would have had to stick to the train schedule, and if he had been wrong about where Hogan was headed, he would have lost valuable time trying to change direction to pick up the outlaw's trail. As it stood, he was pretty sure that he was right about Hogan's being on his way to Texas.

In the morning, Birch stopped back in at the telegraph office and this time was re-warded with a message from Tisdale, who said it appeared that Dunmore's gang was no longer in Colorado. In fact, they had not been seen since the train robbery. Birch crumpled up the telegram in his fist. A bad feeling started to work its way through his lean frame. He was beginning to think that capturing Hogan wouldn't be as easy as he had originally thought.

Before leaving Valverde, Birch made sure he had stocked up on food and water. Jor-nada del Muerta veered away from the river and the shady cottonwood trees that thrived along its banks. Birch guided Cactus among the low, barren hills, the smell of the dark-green creosote bushes strong in the heat of the day. Light-gray desert grasses covered the areas where the creosote did not grow.

He camped out among the hills that night, not bothering with a campfire. The only kindling in the area was the bushes, which smelled awful when burned. Birch had a cold meal of venison jerky, day-old sourdough biscuits, and water from his canteen. Then he settled down for a night under the clear, moonless sky. With no chirps from crickets or croaking frogs to lull him to sleep, Birch lay awake, turning over thoughts of Thomas Hogan in his mind.

Hogan and the gang had gotten away with quite a large sum of money and jewelry — and with the gold bullion, it added up to one of the biggest train robberies to date. But Birch couldn't see how Hogan could travel so fast, loaded down with gold bullion. It was true that Hogan and the gang had probably split the take, but that still left him with about ten bars of gold. Perhaps Hogan was not carrying the gold with him but had hidden it, intending to live off the stolen money and jewelry for a few months until it was safe to go back for the bullion.

Birch tried to push these thoughts out of his mind. It did him no good to imagine what Hogan had done with the spoils. He'd find out soon enough when he caught up with the outlaw.

He closed his eyes. Without a moon, the dark-blue sky was bright with stars. It took him half the night to get to sleep.

By midafternoon of the next day, he was relieved to be in sight of the Rio Grande again. After his lonely vigil the night before, Birch felt reassured to be traveling with an old friend.

He rode into Las Cruces and stopped overnight for a meal, a whiskey, and a good rest. By late afternoon of the next day, Birch was at the foot of the gray granite Organ Mountains. On the other side, crossing into Texas territory, was the little town of Canutillo on the Rio Grande. When he reached Canutillo, he knew he would be home.

CHAPTER 7

Birch rode through a pass in the Organ Mountains and reached the foothills outside of Canutillo at dusk. He chose to set up camp, putting off the inevitable meeting by another day as he spent the night trying to banish some of his demons from the past. He had known when he started out after Hogan that it would be difficult for him to go back to Canutillo. But this was where he had the best chance of capturing Hogan, not somewhere along the way.

At sunrise, Birch sat astride Cactus, staring down at Canutillo from atop a low hill. The town was nestled on the banks of the Rio Grande, less than twenty miles north of El Paso.

A branch of the Texas Rangers had been located in El Paso, and this was where Birch had worked. One of the El Paso Rangers was always stationed in Canutillo. Birch wondered if that still held true, if he would find a Texas Ranger stationed in the town when he got there.

Canutillo. This was the town where Birch had spent his childhood. This was the town where, after his father had abandoned him and his mother, Birch had had to grow up fast at age fourteen. Soon afterward, Birch and his mother had left town. He had never returned . . . until now. Birch narrowed his eyes as the memories flooded in, one on top of the other. The effect was as if someone had thrown open the drapes to let in bright sunlight in a darkened room.

Knowing he couldn't delay the encounter any longer, he spurred Cactus roughly and rode into Canutillo. The place hadn't changed much in fifteen years. It was still a sleepy little border town where all the locals spoke both English and Spanish. In the warmth and stillness of the morning sun, everything had slowed down. Most people had gone indoors to escape the heat, but a few sat in chairs propped up against walls, wide-brimmed hats on their heads, eyes closed against the dust.

Both Mexicans and Americans lived here, working side by side on barren desertlike ranches, eking out a living from the dusty soil. The only thing that seemed to flourish here was cactus.

Cantinas populated Main Street, which was the only street. Drinking was as popular here as it was most places, and because of this, the occasional fight broke out. Generally speaking, however, Canutillo was a peaceful town.

Birch noticed someone slumped in a chair outside the marshal's office, arms crossed, hat pulled down so low that he would have to tip it back by the brim to see anyone coming. Birch recognized the marshal, so he slowed Cactus down and called out, "Hello, Reyes."

The man straightened up slowly, uncrossed his arms, and pushed his hat back. "Do I know you?" he asked. After studying Birch for a moment, he said, "You look like a kid who used to live around here before him and his ma left. Haven't seen him for years."

"How are you, Reyes?" Birch said, leaning forward in his saddle. "You still the marshal around here?"

A smile spread across Manuel Reyes's rough map of a face. "Jefferson, how are you, damn it?"

Birch dismounted while Reyes struggled to his feet. Birch noted that the marshal's paunch had grown slightly bigger over the years, and that his black hair and mustache

73

were now threaded with gray. Reyes shook Birch's hand and clapped him on the back. "You've turned into a fine young man," he said, chuckling. "And of course I'm still marshal. No one else wants the job."

"I would have thought you'd have stepped down from that office by now," Birch replied.

"Hah! Canutillo is a quiet town, same as when you left. Nothing ever happens around here. I'll collect my pay until they carry me out in a pine box." Reyes stuck his hands in his pockets. "So what brings you back here?"

"I'm here on business."

"What kind of business? What do you do for work these days?"

"When I'm not working on a ranch, I take assignments from a man who runs an investigative agency," Birch explained. He felt the marshal could be trusted.

The marshal cocked his head as if he had suddenly latched on to something. "Say, you're not looking for anyone, are you?"

Birch's expression suddenly turned serious. "I'm afraid I am."

He knew the conversation had taken a more official tone when Reyes looked around as if he expected to see eavesdroppers. "Let's get off the street. Come in and have a beer with me."

They shared warm, sudsy beer from a bucket while Birch explained the reason he was there. By the time he had finished, Reyes was looking grave and shaking his head. "He's done it again. Tom swore he had retired."

Birch finished his beer and wiped the foam from his lip. "Tell me, Marshal, I always wondered why you put up with him. Any other lawman would have turned him in long ago."

Reyes sighed. "You of all people shouldn't be asking me that question."

Birch's expression turned to stone. "I stopped making excuses for him when I joined the Rangers and discovered that he was robbing trains for a living."

"How did you know Hogan came back here?" Reyes asked.

"I studied Hogan's pattern of train robbing and figured out that this would be the most likely place for him to hole up. He's familiar with Canutillo, the Rangers are gone because of the war between the states, and it's less than a mile from the Mexican border."

"Before the war began, when the Rangers were still here enforcing the law," Reyes explained, looking apologetic, "outlaws stayed away from Canutillo. Now, we're just a little border town that outlaws pass through on their way to or from Mexico. The only way I can keep the peace is to allow them in here as long as they don't destroy the place." He sighed. "I might not be a hero lawman, Jefferson, but I do a good job of keeping the peace around here."

Birch was silent for a minute, then said, "I'm sure Hogan wasn't the worst of them."

Reyes laughed, beer foam still clinging to his mustache. "That's true. For an outlaw, he has his virtues. For one thing, he lives a quiet life here. In fact, not many of the townsfolk know about his sideline. Other outlaws come and go, some running from the law, some planning a robbery, some headed for Brown's Hole or one of the other bandit hideouts up north.

"For another thing, he's a gentleman. Not like the younger outlaws who think they have the right to shoot up everything and everyone just because they had a couple of drinks and everyone's afraid of 'em. No, Tom's one of the least of my problems. He's never pulled a job near here. Never taken up any other kind of robbery, like banks or stagecoaches."

Birch poured another beer for the marshal and one for himself. Then he leaned forward and said, "Marshal, if you knew where he was, would you tell me?"

"Tom Hogan made his bed; let him lie in it. That's my philosophy. I won't lift a hand to arrest him, but if someone comes into town to get him, that's none of my business. I just find it odd that the bounty hunter is you, is all."

Birch shrugged.

"I'll tell you where he lives when he's in town. . . ."

After thanking Reyes, Birch left with the information about Hogan. He probably could have found Hogan without Reyes's help, but he knew that the law liked to be informed when a bounty hunter came in to take away one of the town's citizens, and this situation was no different.

Birch followed Reyes's directions and rode straight to a small adobe cantina on the edge of town. He dismounted Cactus and tied the leads to a hitching post outside of the building, noting with disgust that there was very little water in the horse trough. The cantina itself was the color of dried mud, not the kind of place that a passing traveler would give a second glance. It was not very well built, with rough wooden posts haphazardly sticking out here and there to reassure a customer that there was a sturdy frame at work here.

After giving Cactus a reassuring pat on the neck, Birch entered the cantina. It took a moment for his eyes to adjust to the darker interior. A young, dark-eyed girl crouched in a far corner near a doorway. She was bent over a large, flat stone that was heated by a small fire. As she turned away from Birch, he could see the beads of sweat that ran down her neck and caught in the small hollow between her shoulder blades, flattening her white cotton blouse against her back. She was making tortillas, taking small amounts of cornmeal dough and slapping it flat, tossing it from hand to hand and shaping it deftly into thin round pancakes before laying them on the stone to cook.

As her hands shaped the next tortilla, she seemed to be aware that Birch was standing and watching her. She gave her head a toss to get her thick black hair off her shoulders, and took a long look at him. Birch took for granted that the arch of her eyebrow was the same as asking him what he wanted.

"I'm looking for Thomas Hogan," he said.

She returned to her work, concentrating on making the dough round and flat. "You aren't the law, are you?"

Before Birch could answer, a gravelly voice called out from the darkened doorway behind her. "You talkin' to me, Lupe? I'm tryin' to get some sleep back here."

Lupe flipped the tortilla onto the hot stone griddle and slowly wiped her hands on a nearby rag. She kept her eye on Birch, her expression impassive. "There's a man here to see you," Lupe said in rapid-fire Spanish. "I'm not sure, but I think he may be the law."

Birch smiled to himself. She must have thought he was a stranger in this town — she probably was born around the time Birch and his mother left. Lupe was also mistaken in assuming that he couldn't understand Spanish.

A tall, gaunt man emerged from the door in the back. Birch studied him with detachment. Mole on the left side of his nose, long jaw. His shock of white hair had been flattened on one side from his nap. He blinked rapidly, as if he was trying to get the gritty feeling out of his gray eyes. The man started hacking, thumping his thin chest with the side of his fist as if that would help.

When he had quieted down, he looked at Birch and asked, "What do you want?" He cleared his throat. In halting Spanish, he asked Lupe to get him a whiskey, then turned his attention back to Birch. With just a flicker of curiosity, Lupe got up and quickly disappeared through the door behind Hogan.

Birch said nothing. He wasn't sure exactly where to begin. The older man peered at Birch, coming closer to inspect his features. "Well, I'll be. Jefferson, is that you?"

Suddenly, Birch couldn't control himself. He hauled off and punched Hogan in the jaw. The older man staggered back just as Lupe came in with a bottle of whiskey and a tumbler.

Hogan rubbed his jaw, his wary eyes on Birch. A wide-eyed Lupe looked at Birch, then Hogan, before slipping over to a table and placing the liquor there.

Hogan's face was screwed up as though he wasn't quite sure what to make of Birch's attack. "What'd you go and do that for, son?" he asked, reaching up to rub his jaw again.

"Don't call me 'son,' " Birch replied evenly. "You haven't been a father to me for fifteen years."

Hogan looked puzzled. "Well, is that any reason to blindside me? Is that what you came here for?" Lupe had paused to listen before going back to the tortillas.

"I'm here to take you in for robbing the Santa Fe line up in Colorado last week." Birch pulled the handcuffs out and grabbed Hogan's left wrist.

Lupe leaped up and ran over. "What are

you doing?" she said loudly. She put herself between Birch and his father and tried to push Birch away. He was unmoved. "He's your father!" she said.

To Birch's surprise, Hogan reached up and turned Lupe around by her shoulders. "Now, girl, I don't want to see you cryin'. I'm goin' away with my s— er — Jefferson here, but I'll be back." When he reached under his shirt, Birch tensed and kept his hand on his gun, but Hogan brought out a handful of money and gave it to Lupe. "You and your mama will have to run the cantina alone for the time being, Lupe. Take good care of your mama. I'll be back. I promise."

Birch wondered if the old man would ever be able to make good on that promise. "Where's the gold, Hogan?" Birch asked.

Lupe flew at Birch, her arms hitting and her legs kicking at him fiercely. "He just wants the gold, *tío Tomas*," she cried. "Run!"

Before Hogan could move, Birch had grabbed her wrists. He held Lupe with a firm grip at arm's length, and watched Hogan to see what he would do. Instead of trying to escape, Hogan gently extricated Lupe from Birch. "Lupe. Be a good girl. I have to face justice someday, and today is the day." He kissed her forehead and turned to Birch.

"I'm ready. You wanted to know about the gold."

Deliberately looking at Lupe, Birch explained, "We'll have to load the stolen money and gold on a train headed back to Albuquerque."

"Aren't we taking the train, too?" Hogan asked with suspicion. His hands became fists and the corded muscles in his neck tightened up and stood out.

The fact was, Birch hadn't thought about taking the train, even though he had considered the notion briefly outside Valverde. Birch tended to feel more comfortable and in control when he was riding Cactus. Traveling by horseback would mean a long time in the saddle, but as much as Birch hated to admit it, he wanted some time alone with Hogan because he was curious about what kind of man his father was.

"So where's the gold, Hogan?" Birch demanded once more, impatiently this time. He chose to ignore, for now, his father's question about taking the train.

There was a short silence. Hogan looked uncomfortable, then seemed to think better of it. Finally, he shrugged and said, "There ain't none."

"What?" Birch couldn't believe his ears. Of course there was gold. Tom Hogan had robbed the train just a week ago. He'd taken a load of government bullion away in a wagon.

"What do you mean there isn't any gold?" he asked again.

Hogan avoided his son's accusing eyes, choosing to look up in the sky, then down to the ground. He scratched his whiskered jaw and, as if he were savoring every word, slowly said, "Well, the truth of the matter is that the gang I run with this time was as crooked as a snake in a cactus patch. Took it all."

Birch shifted his weight from one foot to the other, keeping a careful eye on his estranged father. It was hard for him to believe that Hogan had allowed someone else to get the better of him, especially since he had been robbing trains for almost fifteen years, never riding with the same gang of outlaws more than once.

This was an unexpected turn of events. Birch had planned to come to Canutillo to lay some old ghosts to rest, all the while half hoping his hunch was wrong about his father being here.

Birch now eyed Hogan with distrust. "Took it all, huh? Must've got you pretty worked up, some outlaw you hardly know taking all the loot you worked so hard for."

Hogan licked his dry lips. "Yeah, it did bother me, but there was more of them than there was of me."

"What about that young cowboy that was with you?" Birch asked.

Birch heard a sharp intake of breath from the corner where the tortillas were being made. Out of the corner of his eye, he saw Lupe's face turn pale.

Hogan looked none too well himself. "Well, that young cowboy wasn't runnin' with the Dunmore gang and he wasn't runnin' with me. I just picked him because I needed someone for a job and he was there." Hogan shrugged and muttered, "Didn't ask his name or nothin'."

Birch sighed. Judging from Lupe's stricken reaction, he assumed Hogan knew more about the cowboy than he was telling. Birch had a feeling that if he stayed around for the night, he might run into the young man, but the gold was of more importance at the moment.

Narrowing his eyes and stepping forward with the handcuffs, Birch asked, "Are you sure you're telling me the truth?"

The two men locked eyes for a minute, both too stubborn to be the first to break the stare-down. Finally, still holding Birch's steady gaze, Hogan smiled and held out his arms. Birch clapped the metal cuffs around his prisoner's wrists, snapping the locks firmly into place.

"You coming?" Hogan asked his son, starting toward the back of the cantina. There were two horses, one dun and one roach-backed gray, in a small corral out back. "We'll take Jughead here," he said, indicating the gray horse.

Lupe stood in the doorway of the cantina and watched as Birch saddled Jughead, then helped Hogan up on the horse. He led Hogan around the side of the cantina to Cactus, then they rode slowly out of Canutillo as the lowering sun shone in the sky.

CHAPTER 8

Capturing Tom Hogan had been easy, but it gave Birch no satisfaction. As they rode north along the Rio, Birch thought back to what had happened in Canutillo. Not only had Birch failed to recover any of the loot, punching his estranged father in the jaw had been an impulsive act, not the action of a man in control, a man upholding the law.

But Hogan didn't seem to have held that against Birch. In fact, he appeared to be enjoying riding slowly across the vast, hot wasteland with Birch. He had asked about a dozen questions about Birch's personal life in an effort to find out more about the fourteen-year-old son he had left behind.

"So you're a bounty hunter, are you, son?" Hogan asked.

"I told you not to call me that," Birch said, his voice strained, his jaw aching from the tension he felt, a tension so thick that he could cut it with his Bowie knife and serve it with biscuits.

Hogan looked hurt for a moment, then bewildered. "Well, what should I call you, then?"

"Call me by my name," he replied with controlled effort, "Jefferson Birch." He couldn't resist adding, "You can remember that, can't you?"

There was a small pause before Hogan said softly, "Birch was your mother's maiden name. She must have taken it back after I left."

"No, she never did. I took it after I grew up. When I joined the Rangers," Birch said shortly.

"I heard you'd signed on with that outfit. How is Helen doing these days?"

"She's dead," Birch said tersely. He stared straight ahead. "She and I moved to Fort Stockton a few months after you left. Mama died when I was sixteen."

"I'm real sorry to hear that. Helen was a good woman," Hogan said softly. "Much too good for the likes of me."

Birch bit back the impulse to agree wholeheartedly.

"Tell me something, so— I mean Jefferson. What made you come after me?"

"It's my job."

"Why didn't you let someone else do it?

I mean, why did it have to be you?"

Birch looked sharply at Hogan and answered the question with a question. "Why do you ask?"

Hogan blinked. "Well, it seems to me you wanted to come after me because you bear a grudge agin me, and rightly so."

"I was the only choice. I happened to be living near Albuquerque at the time they were looking for an agent." He waited a beat, then added, "Besides, they put a 'dead or alive' on your head. Another man might be inclined to put a bullet in you so you'd cause less trouble on the way back."

The gaunt outlaw raised his eyebrows as if he was about to say something, but he remained silent for some time.

They hadn't traveled more than ten miles before night fell, but at least they were away from Canutillo, as far as Birch was concerned. They set up camp at the foot of a low mesa near the river.

Birch found a small but sturdy twisted tree and manacled his prisoner to it, then went in search of mesquite wood for a fire. Less than an hour later, the beans and biscuits were cooked and they both held steaming mugs of coffee.

Hogan spoke again. "I never meant to leave you for that long."

Birch chewed on a biscuit, then took a swallow of hot coffee. "What did you mean to do?"

Hogan, one hand still manacled to the tree, put his plate down and began to cough violently, thumping his chest in the same manner as before in Canutillo. Once his fit ended, he managed to pick up his mug and signal for more coffee. Birch poured from a careful distance, in case this was a ploy by the wily old bird to gain his confidence and hurl the hot liquid at him in an effort to escape. Birch wouldn't put it past a desperado like Hogan to do something like that, even if the man was his father.

A few sips of coffee later, Hogan had settled down. He wheezed heavily for a few minutes before he said, "That was the start of my outlaw days, you know. I wanted to give you and your mother the best of everything. That's why we moved to Canutillo. Except it wasn't called Canutillo when we first got there, remember? It was just a little outpost near Fort Bliss." Hogan sighed and stared off into the inky blackness above the Rio Grande. Then he looked back at Birch, his haggard face highlighted by the glow of the campfire. "Do you want me to go on? Do you want to hear all of it?"

From the beginning, Birch had felt nothing but anger toward Hogan, but now he shrugged, looking away from his father. "We'll be together until we reach Albuquerque. If you want to talk, I'll listen."

With no expression on his face, Hogan looked down at his coffee mug. "Okay, I guess that's more than I should expect from you. You remember some of it, I'm sure."

Birch remembered that they had moved to Canutillo because his father had a job as a driver with the San Antonio–San Diego Mail Line, better known as the "jackass line" because they used mules instead of horses.

Hogan leaned back on an outcrop of limestone and said, "We were doin' okay, although my line went from no place to nowhere. Every week, I drove the team from Canutillo to Tucson and back again, deliverin' mail. But the stagecoach mail line went out of business when the railroad was built down through Canutillo to El Paso, and later, beyond. I couldn't get a job with the railroad, because they brought their own people with 'em.

"So I came to a decision one evening and sat you and your mother down to tell you that I was going to El Paso to look for work. I'd send money back to you to keep the ranch going, or maybe to join me when I had a better place. It depended on what kind of work I found. I was hoping to find work on a big cattle spread, maybe learn a few things."

"I remember."

A short silence filled the cool evening air, then the far-off howl of a coyote broke the peace.

Hogan continued. "It didn't work out quite the way I had intended. I went to El Paso at the beginning of the winter season, and there wasn't much work there either. But I heard from an out-of-work cowboy that there were jobs in Silver City up north. He was headed that way, so I went along."

Birch interrupted. "There was nothing in Silver City, was there?"

Hogan fidgeted with his empty coffee mug. "There was supposed to be some big silver-mining operation up there, but I never got that far. See, this cowboy and me didn't have enough money to travel, couldn't even get jobs to earn the money, and the way we seen it, it was all the fault of the railroads. So we stopped a wagon owned by the railroad and robbed it. There was gold on the wagon. Government gold."

He looked up and saw the disapproval in Birch's face. "Oh, see, I didn't mean to keep on robbing. That one time was going to be enough to get to Silver City, but I was caught.

And sent to jail." He said the last two words wistfully: "Five years."

Reluctant to respond, Birch said, "We waited for word from you. Mama was sick with worry. Thought you were dead."

A sheepish expression crossed Hogan's face. "I might as well have been. See, I was ashamed, Jefferson. I knew your mama would hate what I'd done. I didn't want to hurt her. Or you." He looked away. "By the time I got out of jail, I went back to Canutillo and you were both gone."

"We sold the ranch," Birch said, "and moved to Fort Stockton where Mama had some cousins."

"Then you didn't move that far away," Hogan said in a sad voice. "How did Helen — your mother — die?"

Birch tossed his coffee, now cold and bitter, on the dying fire. "I think we'd better get some sleep. We've got to be up early tomorrow to get to the edge of Dead Man's Route by nightfall."

"Jefferson," Hogan used the name pointedly, "I think I have a right to know. Now, you may hate me for what happened in the past, but I loved your mother. I've never stopped loving her, but I guess I figured you two would be better off without me."

Birch's square jaw tightened for an instant. Then, in a dry tone, he replied, "I guess you figured wrong. Until her last breath, she thought you would come back or that she would at least hear from you."

Hogan looked away. "I told you, when I got out of prison, I tried to find you. I wanted to make sure you were both doing all right. What happened to you after she died?"

"When I was seventeen I joined the Texas Rangers in El Paso. I stayed with them for almost ten years. Since then, I've done some cowpunching whenever I wasn't working for Tisdale Investigations."

"Did you ever marry, son?"

Birch did not answer, not even to correct his father when he used the word *son*. Instead, he busied himself with making sure the mesquite fire was out, then said, "It's time to turn in." Birch rested his head and shoulders on his blanket-covered saddle, pushing his hat over his face and crossing his arms.

Hogan's voice came out sounding timid in the silence of the night. "I don't suppose you could loosen this handcuff a bit, could you, Jefferson?"

"No," he replied from under his hat.

"So you're still mad that I walked out on

you and your mother all those years ago," Hogan said. Birch could almost imagine him shaking his head in wonder. "It's not good to nurse a grudge for so long. Makes you do something you may regret later on."

Birch heard Hogan give the manacles a shake for emphasis, but he kept his eyes closed. "Good night, Hogan. Don't take any of this personal. I'm just doing my job. Besides, I'm doing you a favor."

"What favor?" Hogan asked in a sullen tone.

"I'm keeping you alive. Another agent or a bounty hunter would have shot you in the back without a shred of remorse."

A moment later, Hogan's sleepy voice muttered, "Huh, some favor. Being captured by your own son."

Lying in his bedroll surrounded by the darkness, Birch stared at the stars that dotted the night sky. He could hear the raspy breathing of his father, who had slipped into sleep.

Birch turned his thoughts toward the next few days. He would be relieved to get Hogan to Albuquerque and turn him over to the authorities. He knew he should be feeling something more than relief. After all, Tom Hogan was his father. Birch brushed aside the tug of guilt and made a mental note to send a wire to Tisdale when they got to a town tomorrow.

On the edge of sleep, he almost broke into a smile, anticipating the look on Tisdale's face.

CHAPTER 9

Tisdale lay on the bed in his darkened hotel room. A pounding headache and two throbbing feet kept him from getting up. When he had gotten the request from Winslow's agent to come to Albuquerque a few weeks before, he had been curious about New Mexico territory. He had spent the two-day train trip from San Francisco to Albuquerque wondering what it would be like. From everything he had read and from talking to everyone he knew who had visited New Mexico, it had sounded exotic.

But for the last five days, Tisdale had been out in the heat, sweat pouring from every inch of him. It occurred to him that his black flannel suit was probably not the best material for this weather, and he finally broke down and bought a couple of light cotton shirts and vests to wear in place of his more formal clothes. He had felt a bit ill at ease when he first donned such casual attire, but now he hardly thought about it.

Tisdale had done a lot of walking over the past few days. He had tried to hire a buggy when he first got to town, but there was none available. They were either already rented or being repaired. He reluctantly rented a horse, but the stable owner gave him a skittish roan named Buck. Tisdale was not as familiar with horses as he had been back in his cavalry days. He had last ridden a horse when he had followed Birch around Nevada on the trail of an alleged escaped killer. It was only now that Tisdale recalled that it had taken him weeks to recover after that episode.

Tisdale sighed and thought back to yesterday, the first time he had tried to ride Buck. It had been trouble enough to saddle the damned animal, but then he found it difficult to get Buck to stay still so he could put his foot in the stirrup. On his first attempt, Tisdale had found himself hanging on for dear life as Buck trotted down the center of the street.

Now Tisdale was stretched out on his bed, a cold, damp washcloth draped over his eyes. His muscles ached from alternately walking and riding the horse, and his throat hurt from talking until he was parched from thirst. He had never expected that interviewing the witnesses to the train robbery would be such hard work.

Tisdale doubted that he would come back to Albuquerque of his own accord, and he would think twice before coming here when summoned by a potential client.

There was a hesitant knock at the door. Tisdale's headache had subsided a bit, and he rolled over and sat at the edge of his bed. The bed frame groaned under his weight, the horsehair mattress crackled. Another knock brought him to his feet and propelled him toward the door. Upon opening the door, Tisdale realized he wasn't fully dressed yet. He wore only his pants and suspenders. Facing him was Sheriff Gutierrez. Tisdale had the presence of mind to grab his shirt off the nearby chair.

"Sheriff," Tisdale said. "What brings you over here? I hope it's not bad news. Come in." After struggling into his shirt, he turned up the oil lamps. From his visitor's expression, it couldn't be good news.

Gutierrez sat in the chair, his hands flat on the arms, palms down. He didn't say anything for a moment. Tisdale was beginning to think that he was going to have to break out his bottle of good bourbon. Gutierrez just sat there, not saying anything.

"I imagine you came here for a reason,"

Tisdale said as he fastened his shirt.

"Mr. Tisdale," the sheriff started, then paused again. Finally, he asked, "Has your agent located Hogan?"

Puzzled, Tisdale replied, "Why, yes. I was going to inform you later today. I received a wire from Birch just a few hours ago. He's on his way back here with Hogan in custody."

Gutierrez stroked his beard thoughtfully. "Is there any way for you to contact Birch?"

"No," Tisdale answered slowly, "I don't think so. What's this all about?"

Gutierrez rubbed the bridge of his nose and said, "The Dunmore gang. I just found out where they're headed."

"South?" Tisdale heard himself asking.

The sheriff looked disconcerted for a moment, but nodded to confirm it.

"How did you find out?" Tisdale asked.

"A U.S. marshal was passing through Albuquerque on the noon train and stopped by my office. He thought I might want to keep a lookout for the gang. The marshal told me he talked to a bartender in a small Colorado town. The man had served drinks to some of the members of the Dunmore gang two nights after the train robbery. A couple of them got real drunk and got to talking real loud about what they would do to Tom Hogan when they caught up with him. According to them, Hogan tricked the gang out of their share of the loot. Rumor has it that Kane Dunmore's as mad as a peeled rattler." The sheriff let out a short bark of a laugh. "I don't know how Hogan did it, but then again, he walked right past the conductors and porters back in Pueblo, Colorado, when everyone had a description of him."

"So you think that if Birch and Hogan meet up with this Dunmore gang — "

" — your agent is gonna see some lead fly," Gutierrez finished Tisdale's statement. "That's about it." He got out of the chair, his knees cracking with the effort. "Don't know if it's worth anything. Most likely, Birch and Hogan will come in here safely, especially if they take the train. The chances of them meeting up with the Dunmore gang are pretty slim, right?"

Tisdale nodded, then went to the door and held it open for the sheriff. "You know this area better than me. If Birch doesn't take Hogan back on the train, what are the chances of Birch and Hogan running into the Dunmores?"

The sheriff stood out in the hotel hall, adjusting his hat. "Well now, if they're traveling along the Rio, I'd guess they have about a one in two chance. I just hope that if they do run into Kane Dunmore, Birch can take care of himself."

"That's one thing you can count on, Sheriff," Tisdale said with a short nod. But as he closed the door, he began to wonder why Birch had decided to ride into Albuquerque instead of taking the train, which would have saved time.

Then his thoughts turned to Hogan and the gold. He wondered if Hogan was leading Birch to where the loot was.

There might be another reason Birch hadn't taken the train: He had mentioned that Cactus got skittish after a ride on the tracks. Even so, that didn't seem a good enough reason to avoid the train.

Maybe Birch had wanted to delay bringing Hogan to Albuquerque for another reason.

It was possible that Hogan had told Birch he would split the gold with him. But Tisdale couldn't imagine Birch agreeing to that. It was hard for Tisdale to believe Birch would turn bad, but he had known men who had sold their souls for less.

All Tisdale knew was that Birch probably wasn't aware that the Dunmores were on his prisoner's trail. Birch would have his guard up anyway if he had read Tisdale's wire warning him that the Dunmores hadn't been seen in Colorado since the robbery.

Tisdale went over to the washstand and soaked his washcloth, then squeezed out the excess water. His head was pounding again. He would have to trust Birch. His agent had never let him down before. This time wouldn't be any different, would it?

CHAPTER 10

Birch felt a slight breeze stirring the desert as the coffee cooked over the campfire he built as soon as dawn broke. His red-rimmed eyes felt grainy from lack of sleep. This morning, Birch was having trouble reining in his temper. Although he was a light sleeper, he usually slept soundly. Last night, he had not slept well at all. Whenever he began to drop off to sleep, Hogan would start snoring like a choking bull.

He looked over at Hogan, who was still fast asleep. His prisoner's left wrist hung at an odd angle from the handcuff attached to the juniper. A blanket covered him and a rolled-up jacket served as a pillow against the juniper tree trunk. Birch got up and went over to him, nudging his shoulder with his boot. Hogan smiled in his sleep and muttered something that sounded like *Rosemary*.

"Come on, time to get up," Birch growled, standing over his prisoner. Birch reached down and shook Hogan's shoulder.

"Wha— Huh?" Hogan snorted, then reached up with his free hand and rubbed his eyes. He tried to move his left hand, then realized that he was attached to the tree. "Damn! I was hoping this was all a bad dream," Hogan said in a rasping morning voice as he jangled the iron links. He blinked and appeared to focus on his surroundings. Despite his uncomfortable position, he looked wide awake.

Birch had moved over to the campfire and poured a mug of coffee. He brought it back to Hogan. Sipping it slowly, Hogan said, "You got anything to go with this?"

Birch silently went back to the fire and spooned some beans from a pan onto a plate, then added a piece of spoonbread. He unlocked the handcuffs so his prisoner would have full use of his hands to eat. Hogan used the bread to sop up the beans, eating noisily in the quiet of the desert morning.

"So you're still gonna go ahead and turn your own father in?" Hogan finally asked.

"Yes."

While Hogan ate, Birch cleaned and packed up the pans, then doused the fire.

"What made you come all the way down to Canutillo to look for me?" Hogan persisted. "Why'd you think I was there?"

Birch finished throwing dirt on the smoldering fire. He stood up and dusted off his hands. "I remembered hearing you were down there when I was with the Rangers. Why'd you decide to go back there?" he asked in return.

Hogan tossed his blanket at Birch, who caught it and began folding it. "It's the only place I was truly happy," Hogan replied plaintively. "That's where I last had my family."

Birch put the manacles back on Hogan.

Hogan looked up at him with hurt in his eyes. "Why don't you just trust me, son? After all, you're my blood kin. I promise to behave."

Birch gave him a sharp look and shook his head. "I don't believe you." He boosted his father into Jughead's saddle, then mounted Cactus, and they began the day's journey north.

"Are you sure you want to do this?" Hogan called to Birch.

Birch didn't answer for a moment, then turned in his saddle and said, "You sure ask a lot of questions, old man." From behind him, Birch heard Hogan sigh, then he fell silent for a time.

By midafternoon, the two men came to Las Cruces, the town Birch had stayed in overnight on his way south. It looked different in the daylight, a small version of Santa Fe with pale, flat-topped adobe buildings lining the main street, forming a small plaza in the center. Dark-haired women vendors were dressed in colorful calf-length skirts and white blouses, and swathed in head shawls to keep out the sun. Flour paste was smeared on their faces to prevent sunburn, making them look like living ghosts. Birch inhaled the aroma of the cornshuck-and-tobacco cigars these women smoked as they peddled baskets of vegetables, jugs of pulque, and fresh tortillas.

"You onna horse!" a young woman cried. She was no older than Lupe. Birch slowed as she boldly stepped in front of Cactus, her hands on her wide hips. She looked up at him, her black eyes assessing him. "You thirsty? Only a nickel a drink. Half dollar for the whole thing." She held up a squat brown jug.

Birch smiled politely. "Thank you, but I think we'll be moving on."

"Aw, come on, son," Birch heard Hogan say in a plaintive tone. His horse came up abreast of Cactus, and Hogan leaned over to Birch. "Las Cruces makes the best pulque. Besides, I'm hungry. Let's stop and get something to eat. That morning meal didn't agree with me."

Birch relented and dug into his coin bag. He tossed a coin to the young woman, which she inspected before handing him the jug. He would have preferred whiskey, but the agave plant was abundant near the border, so pulque and tequila were the more common liquors around here. He wasn't fond of pulque; he found it to be too sweet for his tastes. But it was obvious that Hogan liked it.

They found a little outdoor stand that served bowls of chili and shots of tequila. Birch dismounted, helped Hogan down from his horse, then ordered two servings and a shot of tequila for himself. The only shade available was on the boardwalk near the buildings. Birch found a recess where they could sit and eat while Hogan sipped from his pulque jug. The chili was so hot that after a while Birch found himself sharing the liquor with his father.

"Damn, this is good!" Hogan said, shoveling another large bite into his mouth. "I don't look forward to Albuquerque. There isn't any place that serves good chili between here and Santa Fe."

Birch set his half-eaten bowl aside and asked, "What is Lupe to you?"

Hogan scraped what was left of the chili

from his bowl before answering. "Lupe is a good girl, very loyal." He caught the look of disbelief on Birch's face and added, "Now don't go gettin' any ideas. She's too young for me, more of a daughter to me than what you're thinkin'."

"That's not what I was thinking," Birch said. "I was just wondering if she was yours. She's about the right age."

"Her mother, Maria, runs the cantina and Lupe cooks and cleans. Maria's a widow, and I kinda look after her and the girl."

"Tell me about the cowboy," Birch said earnestly.

Hogan avoided Birch's eyes, his gaze resting on the uneaten portion of Birch's meal. "Say, you gonna eat the rest of that?" He started to grab it, but Birch was too fast for him. When Hogan grabbed for the pulque jug, Birch took that out of the way as well. "Aw, come on, son, have a heart."

Birch could see that the pulque was taking effect. Hogan was beginning to slur his speech, and he looked as if he was having trouble keeping his eyelids open. Birch wondered if he could get Hogan to tell the truth about the gold by plying him with more pulque, but he immediately dismissed that thought. The truth would come out eventually, without having a hungover prisoner on his hands.

"You tell me about the cowboy and I'll give you back your pulque and chili," Birch replied. He took a sip from the jug just to annoy Hogan.

The prisoner sighed heavily. This was obviously a dilemma for him. "Why do you want to know about him, anyway?" Hogan asked in a grumpy tone, his expression suspicious. "He wasn't nothing special. You aren't thinking of going after him, now, are you?"

Birch took a bite of his chili, keeping his eyes on Hogan the whole time. Finally, Hogan leaned back against the wall, staring straight ahead, a look of resignation on his face. "I don't want you getting any ideas, Jefferson," he said softly. "Don't go after the boy. He's not worth it. Lewis was just trying to earn enough money so he could marry Lupe."

Birch didn't say anything.

Hogan continued, "Lewis kept saying, all the way back to Canutillo, 'I can't believe I did that. Tom, don't ever bring me into one of your schemes again.' " Hogan turned to look at Birch, his expression sober, and added, "He wouldn't even accept any money or gold. Lewis was ashamed of what he done, and I think he's a little wary now of knowin' the likes of me. Ever since we got back to Canutillo, he's been avoiding the cantina, arranging to meet Lupe somewhere else. He's even tried to convince Lupe to stop working at the cantina so she don't hang around me much, but it's her mother's place."

"What is Lewis's last name?" Birch asked.

"Ain't gonna tell you that. You're not gonna ruin that boy's future by puttin' him in jail for somethin' he's already sorry he done."

"I just want to ask him a few questions."

"How you gonna do that from here? We're not turnin' around, are we?"

Birch shook his head. "No. I'd get a Ranger to talk to him — "

"An' the Ranger would have to know why, and you think he's gonna let Lewis go?" Hogan asked, anger and disgust in his voice.

Much as Birch hated to admit it, Hogan had an effect on him. Now he felt guilty about how turning in Lewis would ruin Lupe's future.

Birch reluctantly handed the remains of his chili to Hogan, then sat back, arms crossed, watching him finish it up in between gulps of pulque. When Hogan had set the bowl aside, Birch asked, "Tell me why you are so bent on protecting Lupe and this boy."

Hogan looked away and sighed heavily.

"I guess I owe you that much. Maybe you'll decide not to pursue the matter of Lewis after you know. . . ." He took another sip of the pulque and held it out to Birch, who hesitated, then took the jug.

After taking a long drink of liquor, Birch wiped his mouth with his sleeve and replied, "I can't guarantee anything, but I'd like to know the whole story."

"After I got out of prison, and was unsuccessful in trying to find you and your mother, I gave up. I had nowhere to go and no job, either. I hoped that by staying in Canutillo, I'd hear word from you and your mother.

"I knew that with the Santa Fe Railroad there, Canutillo wasn't likely to become a ghost town anytime soon. And I had hoped that I could find a job somewhere. I did find a job, as a bartender for the Lady Luck saloon. Lupe's father, Felipe, was the owner and Lupe was only about two years old when I started. Felipe and Maria took me in as one of the family. Lupe still calls me her uncle. It made up for missing my own family." Hogan was cradling the pulque jug again, a faraway look in his eye.

Birch interrupted his father's reverie. "I presume that Felipe died?"

"Killed," Hogan snapped. His tone soft-

111

ened slightly. "About a year ago, some Mexican bandits came through town. Lupe was sixteen at the time. She was getting water from the town well. The outlaw leader saw her and wanted her. He grabbed her around the waist, but Felipe was prepared to defend her honor with his gun. Unfortunately, the bandit leader was quicker to the draw."

Birch was fascinated by his father's account. "Then what happened?"

There was a pause. Then Hogan answered heavily, "I killed the leader and saved Lupe. But I couldn't save Felipe. He died a few hours later from a gut shot. Made me promise to watch over Maria and Lupe. Made me promise that Lupe would marry a good man." Hogan looked down, shaking his head. "If Felipe had known what a scoundrel I was, he wouldn't have taken me into his family."

"You never told him?"

"No, I was too ashamed. No one in town ever knew, just like you and your mother."

"Until I became a Texas Ranger," Birch reminded him. He didn't tell Hogan that Marshal Reyes knew of his profession.

Hogan looked at his son sharply. "True." He relaxed his expression and added, "How did you find out about me?"

Birch shrugged and looked away. "I was going through the wanted posters. It was a few years later, the year I married Audrey. Mama died without ever finding out about you."

Birch fell silent, the heat of the day infiltrating the shade of the embankment where he and Hogan sat. He narrowed his eyes and watched the heat shimmer across the dirt road like an invisible snake; the saloon across the dusty plaza looked more like a mirage. He was angry with himself for bringing up Audrey. He hadn't want to give his father any information about himself, other than the fact that he had once been a Ranger. Now Hogan knew something personal, something Birch didn't want to talk about, especially with Hogan.

Birch stood abruptly. "We have to leave now."

To his surprise, Hogan didn't ask him about Audrey. Instead he belched and pounded his chest with his fist. Then he stood up to stretch his arms and legs. "Too bad we have to leave. I think I could get to like Las Cruces."

CHAPTER 11

It was dusk by the time Birch and Hogan reached the edge of Jornada del Muerto. In the morning, they would turn east and leave the Rio Grande, skirting the marshy land that ran almost one hundred miles along the river. Although Hogan had been this way many times as a free man, he saw the land in a different light traveling as a prisoner.

Now he sat, back against a young Joshua tree, his manacles locked onto a low branch. Hogan had hoped that by now, he could have found a way to convince his son to set him free. Barring that, he was hoping to find a way to escape. He was beginning to think it was an impossible task.

It wasn't that he didn't love his son. Just the opposite. He remembered Jefferson having been a good boy when Hogan was around. He had grown into a hard but a fair man, and Hogan was proud of the way Jefferson had turned out. But if he didn't part ways with his son soon, it could mean danger, even death — Jefferson's death. Now the only weapon he had left was the truth.

Hogan looked around him. The campfire blazed bright against the deep-blue night sky. With his free hand, Hogan reached up and plucked one of the large flower buds and handed it to Birch.

"Here, put this on the fire for me, will you?"

Birch placed it on the small grill above the fire, turning it every now and then. After a few minutes, he knocked it off the fire and handed it back to Hogan.

Hogan bit into it. "Ever had one of these?" he asked Birch, who shook his head. "They're sweet when roasted over a fire. Desert Indians eat them as a treat." He reached up, plucked another flower bud, and tossed it to Birch. "Here. Try one."

"Thanks," Birch replied, catching it deftly and meeting his father's eyes for the first time. Hogan felt a swell of pride. Feelings of guilt and regret washed over him as he chastised himself for the thousandth time over not being there to help raise his son, over not trying harder to find Jefferson and Helen. He tried to push those thoughts away by savoring the Joshua flower pod.

The next few minutes were filled with the

sounds of night animals on the prowl and the sound of leathery wings overhead as a flock of bats coasted openly on the smooth night breezes.

"Before we get any closer to Albuquerque, I have something to tell you," Hogan said.

Birch bit into his roasted flower bud. "These are pretty good."

Hogan repeated, "Jefferson, I was hoping that in these past few days, you'd have seen your way clear to letting me go. But I know now that it ain't gonna happen."

"I'm surprised you didn't try harder to escape," Birch replied mildly.

"I know what I done was wrong, but you don't know what you're gettin' into. There are some bad people after me."

Birch stopped chewing, an attentive look on his face, and swallowed. "What the devil are you talking about?"

Hogan jangled the chain links of his handcuffs with impatience. "I'm talkin' about the Dunmore gang. Kane Dunmore, that evil bastard."

Birch nodded. "I know about them. The law up in Colorado is going after them. They've probably been caught by now."

Hogan pounded his free fist into the trunk of the tree. "No, they haven't," he came close to shouting, then thought better of it and explained in a low, urgent tone, "Just before you came into Canutillo, I received word from a friend up in Colorado that the Dunmores didn't stay there. And I'm not surprised that they didn't."

"Why not?" Birch asked, a wary look in his eyes.

"Because I took all the gold, that's why," Hogan said, thumping his chest. "They're after me, the poor sods."

Birch jumped nimbly to his feet and doused the fire with sand and the rest of the coffee. "You cheated them?" he said in a low, fierce tone. He started to pace. "What do you mean, you took all the gold? You told me back in Canutillo that the Dunmores took it all. If you have it, why haven't they come after you yet?"

Hogan could barely make out the shape of his son against darkness, and that was just fine with him. Made him less of a target if the Dunmores were out there. After a moment, his eyes adjusted and he could see Jefferson's features a little more clearly.

Hogan began to tell his story. "See, when I asked them to join me on this robbery, I knew they were rotten to the core. But I needed someone smart to be at the right place at the right time. I timed this robbery down to the minute. But when I was asking around about the Dunmores, I was told that they would bamboozle their own mother if she had something valuable.

"So I figured that into my plan, the Dunmores trying to rob me after we robbed the train. In fact, the night before we put our plan into effect, I went outside for a smoke. I was standing by an open window and heard Kane talking about what he would do to me and Lewis after I helped them get the gold. They were just going to outright kill us."

Birch asked, "What about Lewis? You left him back in Canutillo to face the Dunmores alone if they show up."

"Lewis can take care of himself," Hogan snapped, then added, "He'll be all right. He left Canutillo the day after we got back from Colorado. He's looking for work. Lupe and Maria know about the Dunmores, and they'll warn Lewis."

Hogan continued with his account. "After we got away from the train with the wagon full of gold, we kept going until we were sure no one had followed us. We made sure our tracks were covered, doubling back and all that. When we settled down for the night, I volunteered to take first watch.

"I saw the smug look on Kane Dunmore's face as he agreed. He was certain that he had time to get rid of an old geezer like me. I had already taken Lewis into my plan, and he was willing to go along with me. He knew Kane Dunmore didn't think an awful lot of his abilities as an outlaw, and rightly so. Lewis didn't have much choice, after all — it was either me, or the mercy of the Dunmores. It didn't take a genius to choose which side to be on.

"Since Dunmore and his gang spent most of their time watching me, Lewis was able to slip a sleeping powder into their liquor bottle."

Birch interrupted Hogan. "Let me guess. After they went to sleep, you loaded up the wagon with all the money and left."

"Pretty much. But I also took all their horses and their fighting gear, and hogtied them to boot. I'm betting they got free and were plenty riled up."

"Let me get this straight," Birch said slowly, seeming to have trouble believing Hogan. "You robbed the Dunmores, took their guns and horses, then left them hogtied out in the wilderness. And you think they're still alive?"

Hogan shook his head. "Don't think I'm that cruel. I left 'em a knife to cut the ropes and enough food for a day. They probably got to the nearest town, stole some horses and gear, and are now trying to track me."

"Did they know where you were headed?"

"They probably guessed I was going home to Canutillo," Hogan replied.

Birch was silent for a full minute. Finally, Hogan heard his estranged son sigh heavily and saw him rub the back of his neck. Birch looked up, a sober expression on his face. "Where's the gold?" he asked tiredly.

"Buried," was all Hogan said.

Birch persisted. "Where?"

Hogan shook his head. "I ain't gonna tell you. Not yet."

"Not yet? Why?"

Hogan got tight-lipped. "It's for your own protection, Jefferson. Trust me. I can't explain it now."

"Kane Dunmore sounds mean," Birch replied.

"Mean enough to have a special seat reserved in hell," Hogan said with relish. "From the beginning, him and me mixed like oil and water. It was the dream of all that gold that kept us working together."

Birch tossed a blanket to Hogan, then stretched out, his head propped up on his saddle. "We'd better take turns on watch."

"Fine with me," Hogan replied. He was relieved that Birch was finally able to see his way clear to trusting him. "Loan me your gun." His relief was short-lived.

Birch laughed. "I don't think that would be a good idea."

"You mean you ain't gonna let me go? Don't you believe me?" Hogan asked. "Don't you trust me?"

"I don't know," Birch said thoughtfully. "What you're saying could be true. I tend to believe you, but I wouldn't stake my life on it."

Hogan's tone was full of hurt. "You think I'd kill my own flesh and blood?"

"It's hard for me to say what you'd do. I haven't seen you for close to twenty years."

"How in the blazes am I supposed to protect us if Kane Dunmore finds us?"

"Chances are if he hasn't found us yet, we're probably safe. But just in case, you take the first shift and wake me for the second."

Hogan blinked. "What am I supposed to do if he comes into this camp?"

Birch drew his carbine from his saddle holster, pulled the shells out of the chambers, then tossed the empty weapon to Hogan. "Hold this on him and wake me."

Then Birch settled down on his side, pulling his blanket around him and closing his eyes.

Hogan peered out into the dark desert

landscape, his heart racing just a little faster every time he heard an animal brush against a creosote bush or some sagebrush. It was going to be a long night.

CHAPTER 12

Birch woke up to the sound of whispering. It was still dark, but there was an indistinct glow of dawn at the horizon. He sensed something was wrong. There was another presence in the camp, maybe more than one man. Until he knew how real the threat was, Birch decided it might be dangerous to move. He was suddenly very conscious of his saddle, the smell of the leather that cushioned his head, and of the rocky ground beneath him. It would be difficult for him to get up without alerting the strangers in his camp. So he kept his eyes closed. His back was to Hogan and whoever was making the faint rustling sound.

Carefully, his hand crept around to the other side of his saddle to the holster where he usually kept his carbine. It was empty. He cursed, remembering that he'd given it to Hogan before he went to sleep.

Birch wondered why he hadn't heard anyone enter the camp. Hogan hadn't cried out, so whoever was in the camp probably wasn't unwelcome. He tried to picture the camp layout in his mind. The man probably entered from near the river, on the far side of the camp. It wouldn't have been hard to stay quiet if he'd taken off his boots, Birch thought.

If he continued to play possum, they would pay him no mind. He remembered that his Navy Colt was hidden under his saddle. He might be able to get to his gun. On the other hand, someone could have a gun trained on him right now. With his back to Hogan, Birch had no way of knowing.

Another thought kept him from going for his gun: This might be the Dunmore gang, which would mean there was more than one stranger in the camp. He wouldn't stand a chance against four outlaws, even if his father was on his side.

Birch wondered if what his father had told him last night was the truth, or if he had been making it all up to win Birch's trust. It certainly had done the trick. Birch had started to feel some regard for the man who had deserted him and his mother. He was beginning to see Hogan's side of it. Life hadn't been easy for Tom Hogan once he made the decision to rob a train. He lost several years sitting in prison, and his pride lost him his family. Birch pushed these thoughts aside.

"Where's the key to these handcuffs?" Birch heard someone ask in a mean, flat whisper.

"Probably over there," Hogan replied.

"We might as well kill him," another man said in a low voice.

"Shhh!" Hogan replied. "Don't wake him. And don't even think of killin' him. That's my son."

"You're lyin'. 'Sides, why would that stop me from killin' him?" the second man asked.

In a fierce whisper, Hogan replied, "You damn well better believe I'm tellin' the truth. If you lay a finger on my son, I'll go to my grave without you knowing where the gold is hid."

There was a pause. The first voice finally said, "Better do what he says, Jasper. Don't kill the man. Maybe we should take him with us."

Hogan broke in, sarcasm thick in his low voice. "Oh, good idea, Kane. You think I'm going to show you where the gold is if you bring him along as a hostage? I know what you're thinking. Once you have what you came for, you'll kill me. If he goes along, he gets killed, too."

"How do we get these handcuffs off you, old man?" Jasper growled in a low, menacing tone.

Birch had to think fast. The keys were tucked in a bag on his saddle. He couldn't tell them, but he could shift slightly and hope they would figure it out. He pretended to stir in his sleep, moving away from the bag containing the key.

"Maybe he keeps it in his saddlebag," Hogan said.

There was silence as Birch heard someone creeping up to him. He felt his back tingle slightly, aware that the muzzle of a rifle or revolver was just inches away from his head, aware that his hand had come in contact with his Navy Colt under the saddle, and there wasn't a damn thing he could do without betraying the fact that he was awake.

The sound of the leather flap creaking open, a metallic clink of keys being carefully extracted, then Hogan's manacles being unlocked told Birch that they had found what they came for. He waited for an opportunity, but it never came.

"He sure sleeps sound," Kane said sarcastically, not even bothering to whisper anymore. He must have guessed that Birch was awake. No one used to sleeping beneath a starry sky could have continued to sleep through what had just occurred.

Hogan dropped the manacles with a clang. Birch heard him grunt with effort as he got up.

"I still say we kill him," Jasper said with contempt. "I'll make the old man tell me where the gold is hid. Everyone wants a chance to live."

Hogan wheezed. It took a moment before Birch realized that it was his father's laugh that had turned into a cough.

"Living ain't important to me no more, Jasper," Hogan said through labored breathing. "I'm dyin' anyway. Got lung trouble, got the consumption. And that really is my son over there. No one was more surprised than me when he turned up to take me in. Now let's get goin'."

"Wait a moment," Kane said, his tone full of authority. "We got to do something with this fellow."

"We'll take his horse," Jasper suggested.

"Does he have any other guns?" Kane asked Hogan.

"He has a Colt, but I don't know where it is," Hogan replied truthfully. Birch heard Kane's boots coming toward him. It was now or never. He tensed, then rolled away from the saddle and down a slight decline, still having the advantage of the darkness and a better working knowledge of the area than the Dunmores had. A shot rang out, and he felt the heat of a bullet graze his head.

As he reached up and touched his crown, coming away with a sticky feeling on his fingers, he heard Hogan say in a loud voice, "I told you I wouldn't tell you where the damn gold was if you hurt my boy. Stop it now, Kane, or lose the gold."

Birch felt a little dizzy, but the stinging of the superficial wound kept him from passing out. He was afraid to shoot back, afraid he would hit Hogan by accident.

Kane began cursing at Jasper. "Stop, damn it. If we kill him, the old man won't lead us to the gold."

"Well, what about the young cowboy who was with Hogan on the train?" Jasper shouted. "Why can't we find him and he can take us to the gold? He'd be a lot easier to work with than this stubborn old coot."

"Who you callin' a stubborn old coot, you blasted varmint?" Hogan replied in a raised voice. Birch heard Hogan groan just then. There had been a soft thudding sound, like metal meeting flesh, and Birch figured that one of the desperadoes must have hit Hogan in the gut with a rifle butt.

Hogan moaned. "You didn't have to do that."

"Come on. Let's kill him now," Jasper said to Kane. "We'll get the other fellow."

Hogan laughed. Again, it turned into a hacking cough. "Even if you killed me and found him, let me ask you this: What if I sent him on ahead while I hid the gold myself?"

"You're too weak to move gold by yourself," Kane replied harshly. "Jasper's idea makes sense." Birch heard the click of a hammer being pulled back.

Hogan talked fast and loud. "I'm too weak now, but I wasn't a few weeks ago. Anyway, you'll never know until you kill me, then try to find my friend. It'll be too late if you're wrong. Besides, you won't find him. He's gone across the border with his sweetheart and his share of the gold."

There was an exasperated sound from Kane. "You've got me over a barrel, Hogan. Fine. Here's the deal, old man. You take me to the gold and I won't kill your son." Birch heard the sound of the gun being uncocked. He pictured the barrel end shoved up against Hogan's neck. And there was nothing Birch could do about it short of getting them both killed.

It suddenly occurred to Birch that there

were four outlaws in the Dunmore gang. In all this time, he had heard only two men speak. He wondered if the other two men were just being silent, or had been left behind somewhere.

"You hear that?" Kane shouted to Birch. "I don't know where you are out there, but you keep out of our business. We'll just take your horse and be on our way."

Birch listened to the outlaws and Hogan saddle up.

"Jasper, take his food but leave the saddle. He won't be able to catch up to us if he's hungry and carrying a heavy load," Kane was saying. "We'll meet up with the others. They'll have scouted the area by now."

Dawn was starting to break, a grim gray morning presided over by a pure ray of golden light. Birch could see Kane and Jasper astride their horses, Hogan in the middle. Cactus's lead was in Kane's grip when Birch heard his horse whinny, heard his hooves striking the soft, sandy ground in a nervous prance. Then he saw Cactus rear his head, tugging the rein out of the outlaw's hands. In a flash, the horse turned and started to gallop away. Jasper leveled his rifle at Cactus. Before Birch could sight Jasper with his Colt, Hogan elbowed Jasper's shoulder as the trigger was pulled. The shot went wild. Cactus kept running, out of range of Jasper's rifle now.

With an angry look, Jasper jabbed his smoking rifle into the saddle holster and grabbed Hogan by the collar, pulling the older man half off his saddle. "You did that on purpose. I'll see you die slow, Hogan."

Hogan spat in Jasper's face, then a spasm of pain crossed his face as he started another coughing fit. Jasper recoiled in horror, frantically wiping his face with his jacket sleeve. Hogan righted himself in Jughead's saddle.

Once recovered from his attack, Hogan chuckled. "I'm already dying, Jasper," he said hoarsely. "Wouldn't it be peculiar if you got consumption from being this close to me?"

Without waiting for an answer, Hogan kicked his horse and started north. Birch was aiming for Jasper's back, ready to shoot, when the outlaw suddenly moved out of sight. Kane Dunmore was already over the crest, riding alongside Hogan out of range of Birch's gun.

"Damn!" Birch said softly. He picked himself up from the prone position, but still crouched behind a creosote bush. He didn't know what to think of his father now. The man had saved his life, maybe at his own expense.

In the last few days, Birch thought grimly, I've come face-to-face with my long-lost father, arrested him for robbing a train, then lost him to the Dunmore gang. And now I've just found out he's dying.

CHAPTER 13

Birch spent almost half an hour searching for Cactus. The horse had run nearly a mile in the direction opposite of where the outlaws had fled.

"Come on, amigo," Birch said gently, clucking his tongue and holding out some gray desert grass to the skittish horse. Cactus reached out his long neck and nibbled at the treat while Birch caught up the reins with his free hand. When the horse was finished eating, Birch stroked Cactus's muzzle, then saddled up.

He searched the camp area one last time for anything left behind by the Dunmores, but they had taken all his food and supplies. His stomach rumbled, and he yearned for a cup of coffee, but time was passing and he needed to catch up to them.

He could tell by the tracks that they had turned north, still avoiding the marshy land near the Rio, but he didn't want to take too much for granted. He soon came to an expanse of white sand dunes and knew from the trail that Hogan had led the Dunmore gang a little farther east than he had to go, maybe in an effort to gain more time. If Birch didn't already know that the fine-grained white sand eventually ended in less than twenty miles, he might have given up tracking them. The loose, sandy ground did not hold tracks well.

It didn't take long to catch up to them. The Dunmores were going at a leisurely pace, apparently satisfied that Birch's horse had run off and left him stranded. Birch slowed down, keeping them in sight, but not wanting to blunder into a half-baked rescue attempt.

The ex–Texas Ranger was still a little suspicious of Hogan, even after witnessing him risk his life to save his son. Birch wondered what Hogan had to gain from saving his estranged son's neck. It might be true that he was dying, but Hogan had lied so much to Birch that it was hard to tell the truth from a convenient story. Birch tried to brush aside the thought that Hogan might have some affection for his son. He didn't like to think of it, because he was the one who was bringing Hogan in to hand over to the law for robbing a train.

Birch's stomach growled again, and he began looking for something edible. For what appeared to be miles of flat, monotonous scenery, creosote bushes grew widely spaced apart, with the occasional burst of bur sage or brittlebush.

He spotted a large, ponderous chuckwalla sunning itself on a flat rock and wondered if lizard tasted good. Birch aimed his gun at the creature, but hesitated, remembering that firing a gun might alert the Dunmore gang if they were nearby. As he holstered his Colt, Birch spotted a growth of yucca, the kind with black berries. He stopped and picked a few handfuls, putting some away for when he got hungry later. A few yards away, he spied a couple of screwbean mesquite plants and stripped them of their coiled pods. Eating his improvised meal slowly, Birch savored the screwbean's sweet pulp and the tang of the yucca berries.

Spurring Cactus back in the direction the outlaws were headed, Birch wished his father had given him some clue as to where the gold might have been hidden. He was now certain that Lewis had probably helped hide it. The only way to hide a large amount of gold was to bury it. Hogan might have been in better health a few weeks ago, but Birch doubted that a man Hogan's age would have been able to dig a hole large enough, then transfer heavy gold bars one by one into that hole. Birch figured it was also going to be a long trip to the gold. Once Hogan had drugged the Dunmores and tied them up, he had only one day to find a likely spot and bury his loot before the Dunmores or the law caught up with him.

Birch regretted his decision to ride from Canutillo to Albuquerque. If he had taken Hogan by train, the Dunmores might not have caught up to them. He had justified his reasoning with the weakest of excuses — he just plain didn't like trains — but had eventually admitted that he had wanted time with his father. He had wanted to find out why Tom Hogan had walked out on his family — and he had found out . . . that is, if anything Hogan told Birch could be taken as the truth. But Birch wondered why, once Hogan told him what he wanted to know, he hadn't headed for the nearest town and gotten on a train bound for Albuquerque.

When he first started tracking Hogan, Birch told himself that bringing his father in would keep the old man from being killed by some gun-happy agent. Now, knowing that Hogan was dying, Birch found himself in a quandary: If he caught up to the Dunmores and rescued Hogan, would he turn his father over to the Albuquerque authorities, or would he set him free?

Birch decided to concentrate on the present. If he didn't catch up with the outlaws and get Hogan back, he might not have a dilemma anymore. Birch pulled Cactus up short and stayed on the other side of the sand dune, taking refuge behind a saguaro cactus. He had been spending so much time thinking about other things that he almost hadn't noticed that he had practically ridden right into their camp. He was close enough to see and hear what was happening.

Kane and Jasper Dunmore had gotten down off their horses and were peering into the horizon. "You sure this is the way, Hogan?" Kane was asking, sounding a little suspicious of Hogan's motives. "This sure seems an awful distance from the river, and it don't make a whole lot of sense to go this way if you're coming down from Colorado."

"Well, I didn't go near the Rio for a few hundred miles after I drugged you and stole all the gold. I tried to outsmart you," Hogan replied stubbornly.

Kane walked up to Hogan, who still sat on his horse, handcuffed. He grabbed Hogan's belt and pulled him down onto the ground. Hogan barely had time to cushion his fall with his shoulder.

"Well, I guess you weren't smart enough for us, old man," Kane said, grinning. "You'd better not be trying to stall us, hoping that son of yours is gonna save you."

"And you better let go of me," Hogan replied calmly, "or I'll become a mite forgetful about where that gold is hid." Hogan got up and dusted off his jeans.

Jasper was holding Hogan's horse's reins, the other two outlaws flanking them. It was difficult for Birch to see what the other members of Kane's gang looked like, because their backs were to him. But when they turned toward Hogan, Birch studied them for a moment. He could see that they were definitely brothers, twins at that. Their red hair and fair, freckled skin made them look too young and innocent to be outlaws. Birch recalled their names from the wanted poster: Floyd and Frank Coombes, cousins of the Dunmores. He watched as one twin playfully pushed the other, mocking what had just happened to Hogan.

One of them spoke for the first time in Birch's presence. "Kane, I'm thirsty." It was a soft, high-pitched voice. "We gonna get out of here soon? I don't like this place much." He looked around uneasily.

Birch studied the other twin, who sat with

his eyes downcast. Kane eyed the cousin who had spoken, but addressed his own brother. "Jasper, you mind sharing your water with Frank here?"

"You mean with Francis?" Jasper asked, a look of pure loathing on his face. He opened his canteen and turned it slightly, letting a thin trickle of water pour out onto the ground. "No, no water. I swear, Kane, we should leave these two crybabies here and go find us a couple of real men for gang members." He took a swig from the canteen and sealed it, a defiant expression on his face.

"What about you, Floyd?" Kane asked.

The other twin shrank visibly from Kane's fierce-eyed gaze, then sighed and handed his open canteen over to Frank, who eagerly took a drink. "Don't take it all," Floyd said sharply. "We still have a ways to go, and I don't want to run out before we get back to the river."

"We may even be camping out here tonight," Hogan added.

"Not if I can help it," Kane growled, getting back on his horse and leading the pack. He shouted back, "If we keep moving, we might find some spring water."

Hogan cackled. "Not in this area. There's not a drop of water for miles."

Birch was thankful that his canteens had

been overlooked by the outlaws when they went through his saddle for extra food.

By dusk, Birch had followed them almost forty miles. The Dunmores set up camp in the Tularosa Valley near the foothills of the San Andres Mountains. Birch knew that by midday tomorrow, they would have completely bypassed Dead Man's Route and would be near the river again. He thought about going into the camp tonight and getting Hogan, but there were four of them against him. Besides, Birch reasoned, his father wasn't in any imminent danger. Kane Dunmore wanted that gold and would make sure Hogan wasn't mistreated.

Birch's camp was cold. He couldn't build a fire, because the Dunmores might see it. He wanted a thick steak, bloodred on the inside and charred on the outside, fried potatoes, biscuits, a cup of strong, hot coffee, and a bottle of whiskey to wash the entire meal down. Instead, he gnawed on more yucca berries and mesquite beans. He couldn't even roast Joshua tree flower pods, without a fire.

After washing down his poor meal with canteen water, he settled in for the night, his back against the saddle, his horse munching desert grass nearby. The night was cold and his blanket did little to keep the chill out of the air, but eventually his eyelids began to droop. His last thought before dropping off to sleep was that he had to find a way to rescue his father tomorrow. He wasn't sure he could survive another night out here without a fire.

CHAPTER 14

As Birch had predicted, the Dunmores cut
to the west by midafternoon, heading back
to the Rio Grande. He knew this stretch of
river was unpopulated by towns for almost
fifty miles, but Birch figured that the Dunmores would press on until the sun set. That
would place them in Lajoya for the night.
It was barely a town, but there was a saloon
with a sleeping area in the back for use
after the bar closed down. It might be a
good time for Birch to call in the law.

Birch hung back by a good distance all
the way to Lajoya. It was dark by the time
he got into town. The saloon was the only
place with lights on. Although there was no
sign outside, Birch guessed that it was a
saloon when he saw people staggering out
the door.

Tethered to the hitching post outside the
anonymous saloon were the Dunmores'
horses. Birch moved on down the main street

in search of the marshal's office. When he found it, the door was locked and it was dark inside. When pounding on the door did not bring anyone into view, Birch began to wonder if the marshal was in the saloon as well.

The ex–Texas Ranger wanted to avoid trouble, and he figured the Dunmores were trouble enough when they were sober. So he went back to the saloon, deciding to keep a vigil outside until closing. For the next few hours, Birch kept his eye on the window, watching Kane and Jasper try to outdrink each other. Frank Coombes nursed the same whiskey all night long, and Jasper kept encouraging the other twin, Floyd, to drink more. Birch noticed that Jasper Dunmore treated the twin brothers in completely different ways. He ignored Frank, or if he had to acknowledge him, he did so with contempt. But Jasper appeared to be on good terms with Floyd. Birch wondered what kind of disagreement had caused Jasper to behave that way toward Frank.

Kane interested Birch a great deal. He wasn't as volatile as his brother, but Birch got the feeling that he would rather face Jasper. The outlaw leader might be quiet, but he was clever; he had managed to track Tom Hogan down, and Birch had a feeling that if Hogan's threat hadn't worked, Kane would have had no problem shooting Birch in the back as he lay sleeping.

Hogan sat with the outlaws, looking pale, tired, and miserable. Kane had been plying him with whiskey, probably in an effort to get him drunk enough to let slip where the gold was buried. Hogan hadn't had much to drink, though. His hands were still cuffed, and he kept them under the table most of the time. He wondered if Hogan knew or suspected what Kane Dunmore was up to, or if Hogan was just tired and sick from the day's ride.

The night crawled along slowly for Birch. He longed to enter the saloon, away from the chilly night air, but he waited outside in the alley across from the saloon.

Finally, a short, thin man about sixty years old staggered out the saloon doors. Birch might not have paid attention to him, but the tin star on his shirt caught his eye. "Excuse me, Marshal," Birch said, hurrying to catch up to the drunk lawman.

"Who's 'at?" the marshal asked, stopping and looking around. After turning completely around, he came face-to-face with the six foot ex-Ranger and jumped. "You the one talkin' to me?" Birch nodded. The marshal continued to talk, slurring his words.

"You're a stranger. What can I do for you?" He turned toward his office and started walking.

"There are a couple of outlaws in that saloon. Wanted men in a train robbery." Birch explained who he was and what the Dunmores had done. By the time he was finished, they were sitting in the marshal's tiny office, which was barely big enough for two chairs and a table.

The marshal hadn't interrupted Birch the whole time. He sat with his chair tipped back on two legs, his hands folded across his stomach, as if he were listening intently. But Birch soon realized the marshal had fallen asleep.

He leaned across the table that separated them and shook the lawman's shoulder. "Marshal? Wake up, Marshal." The sleeping man twitched, muttered something, and fell into a drunken stupor.

Rising from his chair, Birch took one last look at the liquored-up marshal before turning and leaving the office. The main street was quiet and dark now. All but one of the nameless saloon's lamps were extinguished. As Birch approached the saloon, he noticed the bartender was still cleaning up inside, the one lantern still burning.

The bartender looked up as Birch entered.

"Sorry, mister, we're closed for the night."

Birch nodded. "I was wondering if there's a place in town where strangers can bed down for the night."

"Two places," he replied. "Here in the back room, or down at the stables."

"I'm looking for a couple of men who came into town earlier tonight." Birch described the Dunmores.

The bartender nodded. "Yeah, they were here until I threw everyone out. I think they went over to the stables for the night. A couple of them were so drunk, they couldn't hit the ground in three tries."

Birch thanked him and left. The stable was next door. He knew that the men were probably sleeping in the hayloft. Small towns like this didn't always have hotels or boardinghouses, so stables and saloons put strangers up for the night for a small fee. The accommodations, consisting of strewn hay over a rough-hewn floor, were usually unsanitary and uncomfortable. But if a man drank enough, he wouldn't notice the smell of rotting hay or the slivers in his back.

The stable's side door was ajar. In a large town, this would have been an open invitation for horse thieves, but in a town where all the inhabitants met at one saloon and got drunk together, it wasn't much of a problem. It was musty inside with the foul smell of fodder, oats, sweat, and horse manure. As he crept along, Birch heard the soft whickers of the horses that inhabited the stalls. His own horse was tethered outside the saloon. Birch hoped there wouldn't be any trouble; he wanted to get Hogan out as fast as possible, but that would be difficult unless he got a horse saddled up for Hogan first.

He found Jughead near the back of the stable and quietly led him outside, all the while listening for the sound of the Dunmores up in the loft. As he was fixing the lead to the hitching post, the muzzle of a gun was jammed up behind Birch's right ear.

"Hold it right there," someone said to him in a low voice. "You thought you were so smart, trailing us from a ways away." Birch turned slightly to get a look at who was behind the gun. It was Jasper Dunmore, smiling wickedly. "You were good, I have to say that. I didn't spot you until we stopped for a few minutes about ten miles away from here."

He took Birch's gun out of its holster. "I should kill you now. I could do it and Hogan wouldn't even know. He'd think you got away."

Jasper chuckled at the thought, and Birch smelled the whiskey stench on the other man's breath. "You couldn't shoot me without waking everyone up," Birch replied.

"Who said anything about shootin' you?" was Jasper's chilling reply. The hairs on the back of Birch's neck tingled. In a clumsy movement, Jasper lifted his gun, ready to club Birch unconscious. Suddenly he jerked as if someone had hit him on the head, then sank to the ground, revealing to Birch the marshal who had been passed out in his office.

Birch started. "How — ?"

The marshal burped, and Birch realized the whiskey he had smelled earlier hadn't come from Jasper, but from the Lajoya marshal, who must have been standing right behind the outlaw most of the time. Birch noted that the marshal was still a bit unsteady on his feet, and he went over to keep him from falling over Jasper's unconscious form. "Sam came over and woke me up," the marshal said by way of an explanation. Birch guessed Sam must be the bartender. "He figured there might be trouble. I hope I helped the right man."

Birch relaxed for the first time in days. He gave a shortened account of who he was and the men he was after. "I have papers in my saddlebags," he said as he picked up his gun and holstered it.

The marshal, who introduced himself as Ed "Frosty" Scofield, replied, "Well, I'll just have to take your word for it. Besides, I heard this fellow talking about killing you, so I do tend to believe you. Now you just help me get him up to my jail, and we'll go see about your other train robbers."

Once Jasper had been safely deposited inside the makeshift jail cell, Birch and Marshal Scofield pondered what to do about the rest of the gang.

"I don't want bullets flying," the marshal warned.

"They're probably all asleep," Birch assured him.

"Maybe," Scofield said slowly, "but this one sure wasn't." They sat silently, thinking about what to do.

"I have an idea," Birch finally said. He laid out his plan.

It took only a few minutes to gather the necessary items to create a small fire outside the stable. They had gotten the stable owner out of bed to watch the fire, which he was doing, nervously fanning the smoke in the direction of the open hayloft window.

"Fire, fire!" Birch called out. The marshal

waited by the side door, gun at the ready. One by one, they came staggering out until all of the Dunmore gang, minus Jasper, was there. Hogan straggled out after them, limping a little and coughing, handcuffed to Kane.

Kane saw Birch first. "You!" He started to draw his gun, hatred in his eyes. Floyd and Frank Coombes looked at Birch with bewilderment, then belatedly drew their guns as well.

"Hold it right there," the marshal called out from behind the gang. "Drop your guns."

The Coombes twins did as they were told. Kane froze, shooting a look of pure venom at Birch. Then he growled low and complied.

With the marshal covering them, Birch searched Kane Dunmore for the key to the handcuffs and let Hogan loose.

Rubbing his bony wrists briskly, Hogan smiled wryly at Birch. "I didn't know you cared so much, son. Thanks for coming to my rescue."

Birch grunted in response, noting how sickly his father looked. It was becoming more and more difficult to see the man as evil and corrupt. But Birch avoided talking too much to Hogan, concentrating on herding the rest of the Dunmore gang into Scofield's office.

When the gang had been crowded into the single cell located in a back room of the office, Birch and the marshal stepped back to survey their handiwork.

"That's a mite pretty sight," he said with a sigh. "I don't think I ever had more than one outlaw in this cell at a time."

Birch nodded, looking dubiously at the stopgap jail cell with its wood-framed door covered by layers and layers of chicken wire. "Will you to be able to keep them here? I could take them with me tomorrow," Birch offered.

"Well now, I think I can manage these fellows without you," the marshal said with a frown. "I'll just get a couple of big, strong men from town tomorrow morning and we'll escort these gentlemen to Belen. The law can take them from there to Albuquerque by train. What about you and your prisoner?"

Birch had told the marshal only half the truth. He had told him about the Dunmore gang, but he neglected to mention what part his father played in the train robbery. Kane Dunmore had been silent until then, but Birch wasn't going to wait around to find out if the outlaw leader could convince the

151

marshal that Tom Hogan was a wanted out-law as well.

After thanking the marshal and bidding him good night, Birch led Hogan outside to Cactus. They went over to Hogan's horse and Birch started to saddle him up.

"What're you doin', Jefferson?" Hogan asked.

Birch made a gesture to keep silent. Hogan didn't say another word until they had both gotten on their horses and started to ride out of Lajoya.

"Now, can you tell me why the marshal didn't hold me as well?" Hogan asked when they were far enough away from the jail. "By the way, where are we going?"

"If you're through asking questions, we're going to Albuquerque," Birch replied. Wea-riness was descending on him as if he were wrapped in a warm blanket in front of a roaring fire. He kept talking to stay awake, determined that they would have to keep moving no matter how tired he was. "I didn't tell the marshal about your part in the rob-bery. I told him that the Dunmores had taken you hostage, which was true enough. I just didn't tell him why."

"And he believed you?" Hogan chuckled. "That story's full of so many holes, I could use it as a sieve."

"I think if he'd been sober, he might have asked more questions. But it was late, he'd just awakened from a drunken stupor, and I think he was just happy to make an arrest on the Dunmore gang."

"They'll be out in a few hours," Hogan predicted darkly.

Birch agreed. "It was only temporary. That cell couldn't hold a five-year-old child with a strong shoulder. I just hope the marshal doesn't get hurt. We'll just have to keep riding all night to get ahead of them. Do you feel well enough?"

Hogan coughed and spat to the side. "I guess so. I'd rather sleep, but then, I'd rather not wake up with another gun stuck in my face." He shrugged, slowed down his horse, and held out his wrists.

Birch stared at him. "What are you doing?"

"You forgot the cuffs. Better make sure a dangerous outlaw like me don't get away," Hogan explained.

The ex–Texas Ranger hesitated, then looked away. "I don't think the handcuffs will be necessary. I'll trust you."

Hogan relaxed his arms and took up the reins again, prodding his horse to go a bit faster. "Mighty good of you, Jefferson. Thank you."

"Did you tell them where you buried the gold?"

Hogan shrugged. "Don't matter now. We're going straight to Albuquerque, aren't we? I mean, if the Dunmores don't catch up with us again before then."

"We could take the train," Birch suggested. "Belen's about an hour's ride. I think there's an early-morning train that goes straight to Albuquerque. When we get there, I'd suggest that you tell the law where the gold is. They may give you a lighter prison sentence."

For a moment, Hogan looked like the mask of death himself. His smile held no warmth or humor. "What will it matter? I don't have much time left anyway."

Birch stared out at the black trail ahead of him. "Why didn't you tell me about your ailment?"

"Would it have mattered?" Hogan asked mildly.

Birch thought about it for a time, then replied, "Probably not. Not when I first met you, at least."

"I wasn't gonna tell you about my consumption. That's why I stay close to Canutillo," Hogan explained. "The air's dry and hot, good for an ailment like mine. I hate having you see me this way. I'd rather you thought of me as a mean son of a bitch than as a pathetic, sick old man."

Birch looked down. "I should have got you on a train and taken you directly to Albuquerque. We would have avoided the Dunmore gang and it would have been an easier trip for you."

"But I wouldn't have gotten to know you as well as I have these past few days," Hogan replied.

As they headed north across the dark, quiet desert, they fell into a companionable silence, each contemplating what would happen tomorrow.

CHAPTER 15

Kane Dunmore paced the cell, which was hard to do considering that there were three other men in there and not a lot of floor space. The twins sat side by side on the one cot in the cell, their legs drawn up on the straw mattress to make more room for their cousin's frenetic movements. Jasper was still passed out in the corner.

Kane made a fist and smacked his open palm. "When I get out of here, Hogan's son is mine. I'm gonna kill him, gold or no gold."

"But Hogan already told you where he buried the gold," Frank pointed out. "So as soon as we get out of here, we just go dig it up."

"*Then* you can kill Hogan and his son," Floyd added.

Kane turned on Frank, who shrank back against the cool adobe wall. "With Hogan and that son of his out there, and us in here, who do you think is gonna get to the gold first?"

"Sorry, Kane," Frank muttered.

Floyd thought this would be a good time to ask about something that had been bothering him since Kane and Jasper told him about Hogan's son. "But, Kane, ain't Hogan's son some sort of bounty hunter? Won't he just take Hogan back to Albuquerque?"

"Yeah," Frank piped in, "then he wouldn't be interested in the gold at all."

Kane sighed as if Floyd and Frank were as dumb as mules.

Floyd didn't like to be treated like that, but he and Frank just listened as Kane explained with exaggerated patience.

"You see, if this fellow is the old man's son, then even if he is a bounty hunter, wouldn't he be interested in the whereabouts of that treasure? All that gold would tempt a priest. I still don't believe that fellow is Hogan's son anyway."

"But," Frank said hesitantly, "why would he make up something like that to save a stranger's life, especially a man who was bringin' him in to the law?"

Kane stopped pacing and looked at his cousin as if he were seeing him for the first time. "There's something in what you say, little cousin. Why would he indeed?" Kane fell silent and continued to pace.

Jasper groaned and stirred. He reached up and rubbed the back of his head, then managed to slide himself up into a sitting position. "Wha' happened?"

"We're in the pokey, Jasper," Kane said sharply. "No thanks to you."

His brother widened his eyes as if he weren't focusing on anything, then shook his head as if that would take care of the problem. Then he slowly stood up. "Jail? I thought I had that son of a bitch. I was gonna take him outside of town and leave his body for the vultures."

"That meddling town marshal brought you in," Frank said with relish. "You've been out almost two hours."

"You okay?" Floyd asked. He wished he could get up and pace in place of Kane. His legs were starting to ache from not being able to stretch them.

Jasper felt his jaw for stubble, then looked over at Floyd. In a surprisingly mild tone, he said, "Yeah, I'm fine now." He crossed to the one window in the room, a small, high opening too small for a man to fit through. "How we gonna get out of here?" he asked.

Kane grinned. "I thought you'd never

ask." He grabbed the wire layers on the cell door and pulled. The wire gave a little. He tugged harder, and it started to come off the frame. Floyd and Frank's worried expressions melted into relief. Jasper let out a laugh.

"Why didn't you do this sooner?" he asked his brother.

"Why, Jasper," Kane said, reaching over and patting his brother's cheek, "we were waitin' for you to get your beauty sleep."

All four men crowded over to the cell door and began pulling at the wire until there was an opening large enough for a man to climb through.

When they were all out, they didn't have to search far in the marshal's office for their guns. They found their guns hanging by their gun belts on the pegs that stuck out of the adobe wall. While the four outlaws were strapping their guns on and checking for bullets, Floyd looked out the window. It was nearly dawn, still too early for many townsfolk to be up and about. He hoped they could get out of town without any bloodshed.

"What's it look like out there, Floyd?" Kane asked.

"All clear, Kane. We just gotta get our horses from the stable and we can probably be out of town before the marshal gets done shaving."

Floyd tried the door. "It's locked," he said. "From the outside, I think."

"Of course it is," Kane said. "He wouldn't be much of a lawman if he didn't lock his office door at night." He came over and examined the door.

Jasper went over and tested the door for sturdiness. "I don't think this is much stronger than that cell door. Come on, I need some help." Floyd and Frank put their shoulders to the door, trying to push it open. The door groaned, giving a little.

Kane finally cleared everyone out of the way and gave the door a firm kick. It swung wide open, now twisted, the lock barely hanging on the frame.

Keeping to the shadows and hugging buildings, the four outlaws crept over to the stable. Inside, they quickly saddled their horses and unlocked the stable door. Once outside of Lajoya, Kane turned to the others and said, "I'd've liked to stay long enough to teach that marshal a thing or two before killin' him, but we got to get to the gold before Hogan does."

"Kane, I don't mean to keep asking questions," Floyd said, "but they got a two-hour head start on us. How we gonna get there before they dig up the gold?"

"We can make up some time if we take the train," Kane replied.

Jasper was frowning now. "But what if they had the same idea and we end up on the same train as them — won't they see us?"

Kane thought about that. "We're about an hour away from Belen, where we can catch the morning train. There'll be at least two passenger cars. We stay out of sight, and watch for them, then board whatever car they ain't on."

That seemed to satisfy everyone. A silence fell over them, but it didn't last long.

"What if he told us wrong, Kane?" Frank asked. "I remember you tellin' us not to kill him yet because he might've been lyin'."

Kane straightened up in the saddle and stared straight ahead, his jaw set. "Then I'll hunt him down and kill him, whether he's sick or not. No one makes a fool of Kane Dunmore and lives."

"That's right, Kane," Frank said in agreement. "No one makes a fool of you twice."

Kane turned and gave his cousin a hard stare. Floyd reached out and hit his twin in the arm. As the meaning of his words sank in, Frank reddened and muttered, "I didn't

161

mean it that way, Kane. Honest."

"Sure you didn't," Jasper said in a sarcastic tone, "Francis."

CHAPTER 16

Marshal Scofield was in a good mood when he woke up the next morning. He didn't feel as lousy as he usually felt after a night of hard drinking, which was just about every night. Of course, it wasn't every day that he had four wanted outlaws enjoying Lajoya hospitality in his temporary jail cell. He had insisted on having the cell built until there were enough funds for the town to build a real jail.

Scofield dreamed of the day when he would have two cells with real metal doors on them and keys to lock up the outlaws that he envisioned coming through town. As he dragged a straight razor across his whiskers, he made a note to take some breakfast to the prisoners.

Half an hour later, he had persuaded his neighbor, Mrs. Packard, to make the prisoners' morning meals. With four hot plates of food packed in a large hamper, Frosty

Scofield made his way over to the jail. Although he distinctly remembered locking the front door the night before, he noticed that it was ajar. When he got up close, he realized that the door had been kicked open. The metal lock was hanging on the outside of the door frame by a splinter of wood.

"I got some breakfast for you, fellas," he called out. No one answered, not even with a string of swear words.

He set the hamper on his table, which served as a desk, and went back to the cell. The sight that greeted his eyes nearly tore his heart out. The layers of wire that had been nailed firmly in place were now torn from the wooden door frame. The prisoners were all gone. The marshal walked into the cell, took his hat off, and sat on the cot.

"Damn!" he muttered under his breath. He brushed his hat across his leg in a gesture of frustration.

Scofield had been looking forward to escorting the Dunmore gang to Belen. Now he would have to send a wire to the lawmen in towns along the Rio Grande. One of them might spot the gang. Scofield remembered something Birch had said last night: The Dunmores were trying to find a cache of gold buried somewhere in New Mexico. He would have to find out more about the gang's last robbery.

The disappointed marshal got up from the cot, shaking his head. As he passed the table with the hamper on it, he reached inside and grabbed a biscuit. Might as well not let all that food go to waste.

Birch woke up in his room at the Belen Hotel to find Hogan quietly getting dressed, his back to the bed. When he had finished putting his boots on, he sneaked a look back at Birch, who quickly closed his eyes to feign sleep.

Hogan got up off the bed carefully and began to open the door as quietly as possible. Birch waited until Hogan was about to slip out the door before saying, "Maybe I should have put the handcuffs on you last night."

Hogan froze in the doorway, then his shoulders relaxed and he replied, "Well if that's the way you feel — " He turned around and held his arms out to Birch. "Can't blame a man for tryin'."

Ignoring the theatrics, Birch got up off the bed and splashed some water on his face. "We should have enough time to get a decent meal this morning before getting on the train. We'll be in Albuquerque by late morning." He paused, then turned to face Hogan. "I think I can guess the reason you didn't object to traveling up the Rio Grande by horse."

Hogan looked sheepish.

Birch continued, "You made it clear enough that you were hoping I'd let you go of my own accord. I want you to know that I fully intend to bring you in." He started for the door, then turned around to point a finger at Hogan. "Don't try another escape."

Hogan shrugged, doing his best to look innocent. "What escape? I was just gonna look for the outhouse. A man has a right to answer the call of nature, don't he?"

Birch gave him a hard look, obviously not believing him. They went down to the hotel restaurant, a small dining room off the lobby that served strong black coffee, biscuits, and sausage gravy. Birch was so hungry, he had two helpings of biscuits and gravy.

Hogan, on the other hand, left half his meal untouched and pushed back from the table, watching Birch eat. "You're eatin' like a post hole that ain't been filled up," he said.

Birch paused to chew and swallow before answering Hogan. "When I was following you and the Dunmores, I had to forage for my meals. If I ever see another yucca berry, it'll be too soon."

While they were drinking their last cup

of coffee, the town marshal came in and sat down at the next table. He opened a newspaper and read while waiting for his meal.

Birch looked at a schedule that he had picked up at the train station earlier. "The train should be arriving in a few minutes. We'd better get out of here."

A young boy came into the dining room and walked up to the lawman at the next table. He handed him a piece of paper. "Marshal, you got a wire from the marshal at Lajoya. Some outlaws were in his jail and got loose."

The marshal laughed. "That's no surprise, son. You ever seen that excuse of a jail?"

The lad shook his head solemnly, but the marshal had already turned his attention back to his paper and coffee.

Birch and Hogan looked at each other, then Birch paid for their meal and they left the hotel.

"So, are you still going to take me to Albuquerque?" Hogan asked as they got on their horses.

"Well, no reason not to," Birch said.

As they rode their horses to the train station, Hogan said, "Jefferson, I sort of didn't tell you the truth last night."

"About what?"

"Well, about telling Kane Dunmore where

the gold was buried."

Birch turned in his saddle. "You lied to me?"

"Well, it wasn't exactly lying. I just didn't tell the whole truth. You asked if I told them where the gold was buried and I answered, 'Don't matter much now,' if you recall."

Birch groaned and pulled on the reins to stop Cactus. Hogan pulled up next to him. "So do you want me to show you where it's buried now?" he asked.

"I should just wire ahead to Albuquerque and let someone else go after the Dunmores," Birch said reasonably.

"You're right, Jefferson. That's what you should do."

Birch looked at Hogan with suspicion. "Tell me one thing: Why didn't they kill you when you told them?"

Hogan's expression brightened for a moment. "Most of 'em wanted to leave me dyin' in the desert. But Kane, he's sharp. He pointed out that I might be lyin' and if they killed me before finding the gold, it wouldn't be too smart."

"Why did you change your mind and tell them where the gold was?" Birch asked.

Hogan sighed, a weary look on his face. "I really am dyin', son. I guess at one point in the desert, I just wanted 'em to get it over with. Kill me quick."

The ex–Texas Ranger studied his father, then said, "Why are you telling me this — you want me to go after the gold now? Or is this just another trick to delay going to Albuquerque in the hope that you'll be able to get away?"

Hogan threw an innocent look at Birch. "Would I do something like that? Haven't I been cooperative lately?" Then he turned serious. "Besides, I'd rather die trying to stop the Dunmores from getting all that gold than to go to prison with the knowledge that they're out there free, livin' it up at my expense."

Birch thought about it. Tangling with the Dunmore gang again would be extremely dangerous. He wasn't concerned about himself — it was his duty to the client to recover the gold if he could. But Hogan might not survive another run-in with the Dunmores. Putting himself in his father's place for the first time, Birch realized why the old man would rather put himself in a risky situation than go to prison. Still looking warily at Hogan, Birch nodded. "All right. We'll go after them."

"Great," Hogan replied, looking exultant. He put out his hand expectantly. "Now, can you lend me a gun?"

Birch's eyes narrowed. Hogan put his hands up in a gesture of surrender. "Okay, no gun. When we run across them, I'll just distract them for you by having 'em shoot little holes in me while you sneak up behind 'em."

"You know, Hogan," Birch replied, "sometimes you can be real spiteful."

Hogan's eyebrows shot up in surprise as he looked at Birch. Then Birch smiled, just a little.

CHAPTER 17

As they boarded the train for Albuquerque, Hogan shifted his eyes from porter to conductor to passenger. Whenever someone looked at him, he averted his eyes, turning away so they couldn't catch a glimpse of his face. Hogan leaned toward Birch and in a fierce tone, whispered, "You told me you wanted to go after the Dunmores."

"We are," Birch replied. "Just relax. You're acting like you plan to rob a train."

"That's not funny," Hogan snapped, shifting his eyes around. "Someone might overhear you."

Hogan grabbed Birch's sleeve and said, "But this train goes to Albuquerque. If we get off there, someone is bound to recognize me."

"We're getting off after Albuquerque," Birch replied. "This should put a few miles between us and the Dunmores. I should have done this in the first place, but I don't like trains much."

Birch hoped the cell had held the gang long enough for Birch and Hogan to get to Belen and board the train. When they reached their destination, they would have to look over their shoulders constantly. Getting to the place where the gold was buried was one thing. Whether they were alive after they got to the gold was an entirely different matter.

The train lurched forward, picking up speed as it left the depot.

Hogan settled back in his seat. With a smile, he replied, "Like they say, the acorn didn't fall too far from the tree."

"What do you mean by that?"

"Well, the railroad took away my job, and I never forgave 'em. Even went to jail for it. And then I find out you don't like trains. Must run in the family."

Birch gave Hogan a hard look. He didn't like being compared to him. "I prefer to be out on the trail. When I'm on a train, I feel kind of trapped. That's why I don't travel on trains much. And I'm not sure there's a comparison between my dislike of trains and your hatred for the railroad company because you blame them for all the hardships in your life."

Hogan grew sober as Birch ended his lecture, fell silent, and turned away from his charge. After a while, Hogan replied, "You're surely right, Jefferson. I apologize."

"Tickets," the conductor said as he came by. Birch handed two tickets to him. The conductor did a double take, then said, "Say, aren't you the agent that talked to me about a week ago? My name's Murchison, Ned Murchison."

Birch could do nothing but acknowledge that he was the agent. They shook hands, Murchison casting a suspicious glance at Birch's companion, who had pulled his hat over his face. Finally, reluctantly, the conductor moved on to the next passengers and Hogan breathed a sigh of relief. "Thanks for not saying anything, son."

"Don't call me that," Birch replied in a testy tone.

"Sorry, I forgot," Hogan muttered.

The next time Murchison came around was when the train was pulling into Albuquerque. Birch asked him if he would be staying with the train past this stop. "No," the conductor replied. "I'm just filling in for someone today. Another conductor takes over from here. My home is in Albuquerque."

"Then maybe you can do me a favor," Birch replied.

Murchison nodded. "Be glad to."

Birch wrote a note, folded the paper, and handed it to the conductor with instructions. "Take this to Arthur Tisdale at the Stratford Hotel. If he's checked out, take it to Sheriff Gutierrez, and make sure he informs Russell Winslow of my plans."

The conductor tucked the paper in his pocket and shook Birch's hand again. "I'll make sure someone gets this within the hour."

"Thanks."

The train pulled out of the station a few minutes later, heading north to Santa Fe. Birch intended to stay on the train until they reached Raton, near the Colorado border. The scenery gradually changed from scrub desert and low, bare mountains to lusher, greener hill country. There were more trees, although many in the valleys were still scrubby. Mesas began to crop up, and tall fir trees clung to the sides of high, gray mountains.

As the train passed Santa Fe, Birch wondered if they had outrun the Dunmores. The only way for the gang to get to Raton at the same time would be if they were on the same train. Birch didn't think there was much of a chance of that.

Hogan's mouth was slack from sleep. Birch

studied him, noting how thin he was. Back in Canutillo, he hadn't known Hogan that well, and it never entered his mind that the man might be ill. Looking at him now, Birch thought he could see a grayish cast to his skin. Hogan broke into a coughing fit, but never completely woke up.

He had heard people say many times that they were lulled to sleep by the rhythmic clacking of the tracks underneath the iron horse. But Birch had never been able to sleep on a train. With one last glance at his charge, he settled back and watched the landscape roll by.

It was mid-afternoon when the train rolled into the Raton station. Birch shook Hogan's shoulder; Hogan awakened with a snort and a coughing fit. "We there yet?" he managed to ask in a sleep-rough voice.

Birch's eyes felt gritty and raw. He blinked a few times, hoping there was a public water duct where he could splash some cold water on his face. "We're there. Come on."

They found their horses waiting for them by the cattle transport car. Birch had taken the saddles with them on the passenger car. He saddled up Jughead and Cactus and the two men rode down Raton's main street.

With trade coming in not only from Colorado, but Oklahoma and Texas as well,

Raton was a busy town. Trading posts, general stores, and saloons were housed in sand-colored adobe buildings and people seemed to be bustling purposefully in every direction.

Hogan pointed to a little restaurant in one corner of the main plaza. "Let's eat there."

Once Birch had some hot coffee in his system and a plate of beans, bacon, and biscuits to work on, he felt a little less like a train running on an empty firebox.

Hogan cleaned his plate, sat back in his chair to stretch his arms, and took a deep breath. "Ah, I feel well rested."

A bleary-eyed Birch sipped his coffee, seeming to take no notice of Hogan. Finally, he set his coffee down and stood up, tossing a few coins on the table to pay for the meal. "Let's go."

"We gonna get a hotel room for the night?" Hogan asked.

Birch smiled wearily. "Not if I can help it. The Dunmores are still on our trail, from what you've told me." He waited for Hogan to tell him that he hadn't really told Kane Dunmore where the gold was, but Hogan remained silent. With a sigh, Birch continued, "So that means we've just got to head out of town and hope we can find the gold before they do."

They left the restaurant and got back on their horses. Birch rode slowly down the street until they came to a stable. He turned to Hogan. "Do you want to stay here with the horses or come in with me?"

"What're you gettin' here?"

"A wagon to load the gold onto."

Hogan's face took on a sly expression. "Oh, I'll stay here with the horses."

Birch nodded silently and started to take out the manacles. Hogan looked hurt. "What're you doin' with those things?"

Birch looked up, his face impassive. "You said you wanted to stay here with the horses. I can't let you out of my sight unless I cuff you to the hitching post."

His shoulders slumping in defeat, Hogan sighed. "I'll go in with you."

They hitched Hogan's horse and a horse from the stable to the wagon. Birch wanted to keep Cactus free.

"We'll also need tools for digging," Birch said. "What about other supplies? Are we far from the location?"

Hogan shook his head. "It's only a couple of hours' ride from here."

They ducked into the general store next door and bought two shovels, several lanterns to light their way at night, and a large square of canvas. Once outside, the two men loaded the items into the buckboard. Hogan was given the reins and Birch stayed on his horse, riding by the side of the wagon.

As they headed out of Raton, Hogan stayed quiet, except for an occasional sidelong glance at Birch. "I have to tell you, Jefferson, sometimes I'm not sure what to think about you."

"What does that mean?" Birch asked.

"Well, here I am, only known you a few days. I know you're my son and I know you were a Texas Ranger, but even Rangers have been known to go bad," Hogan explained. "Out here in the middle of the desert alone, and me clapped in those infernal manacles, you could take the gold for yourself."

Hogan's face was eerily underlit by the lantern he carried, but Birch could see that he was looking at him with a little apprehension.

"So you think I'm going to kill you?" Birch said slowly.

Hogan looked straight ahead and said in a surprisingly strong voice, "The thought had crossed my mind."

Birch made an impatient sound. "But why would you think that?"

"Gold does strange things to a man. I've seen a man kill his brothers for gold."

Birch didn't say anything for a while. Finally, he said, "You're going to have to trust me, Hogan. That's all there is to it."

"I'll tell you what, Jefferson," Hogan replied. "I'll trust you as much as you trust me. When we get out there, don't be offended if I don't turn my back on you when the digging starts."

"I think you've got more to worry about with Kane Dunmore on our trail than me doing you in for gold," Birch replied in an acerbic tone. The two men fell silent, watching the land flatten.

Birch noticed that they were headed west, back toward the Rio Grande. When they entered a small canyon, dusk had given way to night. Birch lit two lanterns, which seemed to give the darkness an unnatural glow. He studied the red basaltic walls of the canyon as they closed in on both men.

Just as Hogan no longer trusted Birch, Birch had little reason to trust Hogan. It occurred to him that Hogan might have struck a deal with Dunmore and was leading Birch into an ambush for a chance at some gold. But he quickly dismissed this notion, remembering that Kane Dunmore ran when he had the chance to save his brother, or to kill his betrayer, Hogan. No, Dunmore was as dishonest as they come, and Birch knew that Hogan was aware of this.

The canyon had narrowed until they had

barely enough room for the wagon to pass, Birch leading. He was past tired now. In fact, he had his second wind and felt as if he'd turned in early and gotten a normal night's rest.

The canyon suddenly opened out, a wide expanse of starlit country with several mesas in sight. The moon lit up the landscape with a pale, cold light. Birch was just about to ask Hogan how much farther they had to go when Hogan slowed the wagon and looked up. Following his gaze, Birch saw that the nearest mesa was almost a low hill with a labyrinth of pueblo ruins at the crest. Without turning around, Hogan said, "Up there. It's up there."

They stopped at the foot of the mesa, listening to the silence that encompassed the adobe wreckage. And in that moment, Birch heard the faint but unmistakable sound of horses doggedly galloping toward them.

CHAPTER 18

The sound of riders behind them resonated off the narrow canyon walls. The echo made it seem as if the pursuers were right on their heels, but Birch was aware that who- ever was behind them probably wasn't that close. Still, Birch didn't want to take a chance. He urged the wagon's horses forward at a gallop. Hogan barely managed to hang on to the reins and his seat at the same time. Birch and Cactus stayed with the wagon horses until they reached the foot of the mesa.

"Quick! Get out of the wagon," Birch said in a low, urgent voice. "If we hurry, we can get to the ruins for shelter."

"What, and leave the shovels?" Hogan said. "Whoever's behind us is probably lost by now. That canyon can deceive people."

Birch looked around for a place to hide the wagon and horses, but the land was barren of any form of shelter, except the pueblo that sat at the top. There was no time to drive the wagon up there. Birch considered bringing the wagon around the mesa to hide it. "Never mind the shovels," Birch replied firmly. "How long would it take to get to the back of this mesa? Is it as steep as the front?"

Hogan shrugged. "It's easier to climb, which is how I got the wagon up here last time. But it takes about half an hour to get there."

Birch looked back toward the canyon. "We may not have the time. Climb on down from there. We'll just have to get up this way. If that's the Dunmore gang, I want the advantage."

Hogan jumped down from the wagon and Birch grabbed his wrist, swinging the older man up onto the saddle.

"You sure this horse can hold the two of us?" Hogan asked doubtfully. "This mesa may not be as high as some, but it's plenty steep."

"Cactus can take us both. We'll worry about the wagon later."

Cactus climbed the mesa nimbly, reaching the top in less than five minutes. At the top, Birch and Hogan dismounted and crouched behind a crumbling adobe wall that gave them a view of the path they had just taken. A trail of dust was the only visible evidence of the visitors who were approaching. Birch peered around, tensing at the thought of the gang that had pursued them since Jornada del Muerta. If Kane Dunmore escaped from the Lajoya jail, then somehow he had found a way to follow Hogan here.

Four tiny figures emerged from around a bend below them. In the bright moonlight Birch was able to single out Kane Dunmore from the rest of the gang. Kane had noticed the wagon and was circling it, inspecting it for evidence of who had been traveling in it.

Finally, he shouted, "Hogan! I know you're up there. We can wait here as long as you can."

"What're we gonna do, Jefferson?" Hogan asked, fidgeting anxiously. He was pale and sweating. Birch was relieved they hadn't had to climb one of the higher mesas.

Hogan's breath was coming in such short gasps that Birch wondered if this was another sign of consumption. Hogan's manacles clanked when, in his crouched position behind the crumbling wall, he moved his arms to steady himself.

A rifle shot rang out, the bullet chipping off a nearby bit of ruined adobe wall. Birch looked around. There was a small circular pit behind them, about four feet deep.

"Here," he said, taking Hogan by the arm. "You stay low. I'll get my carbine and scare them off." I hope, he added silently.

Birch slipped the loaded Spencer repeater carbine out of its saddle holster and went back to his post. He checked the number of shells in the accompanying box; there was only half a box, enough for a couple of extra rounds. Birch knew he wouldn't be shooting to kill, since carbines had a shooting distance of up to five hundred feet and the Dunmore gang was too far away.

The Dunmores had taken cover behind the wagon, taking shots up the hill at Birch and Hogan to keep them pinned down. When Birch leveled the Spencer and squeezed the trigger, the carbine jammed. He threw down his weapon, muttering a few curses with bullets whizzing around his ears, and drew his Colt. It was an even less accurate weapon, but he had no choice. He returned fire.

Studying the ruins while he reloaded the Colt, Birch noticed that there were several almost complete rooms on the other side of the mesa, about seven small circular pits, with one large round pit in the middle. Small square rooms seemed to be built around the edge of the mesa, encompassing the pits. It was clear to Birch that at one time, the circular pits had been rooms as well — perhaps for community gatherings. The walls were crumbling, but Birch could see that the walls had been high enough to accommodate people, and in the center of the circles was an indentation as if for a fire.

Birch turned his attention back to the Dunmore gang. After spending the second round, he was loading up again when he realized that he had been shooting at only three men. One of the Dunmore gang must have broken cover, intending to go around the hill and ambush him from behind. One of the twins stood up from behind the wagon for a better shot with his rifle. Birch aimed and fired. The twin went down, clutching his shoulder and dropping his rifle. Meanwhile, another bullet whined past the left side of Birch's head, the heat so intense it felt as if his ear had been brushed with a branding iron.

"Anything I can do, Jefferson?" Hogan was at his elbow now, his bound hands reaching out. "Two guns are better than one."

Another round of fire, much closer this time, decided Birch. He unlocked Hogan's handcuffs and placed the carbine in his hands. "If you can fix this, keep firing at them while I make my way down the hill." He studied the area and realized that if he stayed low, there was enough cover to take the rest of the gang by surprise. Hogan pulled on the lever in front of the trigger. "You jammed the magazine cutoff," Hogan explained. He gestured with his head toward the east. "Go!"

As his father returned fire, Birch began to creep down the hill, weaving his way through the ruined pueblo structures. He could faintly hear a man cry out as if he'd been hit. Birch hoped it wasn't Hogan. Pausing for a moment to listen, the sound of the Spencer could still be heard. If Hogan had been hit, it wasn't too bad.

Just as he reached the bottom of the hill, Birch came face-to-face with a mean-looking man with a perpetual sneer. This was Jasper Dunmore, Kane's brother. He aimed his gun, and just as he fired, Birch half slipped, half dove onto the ground, rolling out of range. Jasper's shot missed. Birch grabbed a rock and threw it at the outlaw, catching Jasper right above his left eyebrow. Surprised and stunned momentarily, Jasper regained his balance, dropped his gun, and tackled Birch. The two men fell on the rocky ground, grappling for each other's throat.

Jasper threw a punch that glanced off Birch's head, leaving him stunned. While Birch gathered his wits, the outlaw scrambled off in search of his weapon. When Jasper found his gun, he turned around to aim at Birch again. Just before he squeezed off a shot, Birch rolled behind an outcropping of rock to safety. He reached for his Navy Colt, only to find an empty holster. Thinking back, he realized that his gun must have been lost during his struggle with Jasper.

Birch could hear Hogan still shooting and Kane returning fire. Peering out from behind the rock, he could see Jasper cautiously heading toward him. Birch had no weapon except the Bowie knife stuck in his boot. He unsheathed it and examined it. Although he'd heard of men who could throw a knife with deadly accuracy, he'd never practiced. The only thing he'd used the knife for was skinning rabbits before cooking them, and occasionally to defend himself against another man who didn't have a gun in his hand.

"I know you're behind there," Jasper called out in a raspy voice. He was out of breath from their scuffle. "You don't have a gun. I can see it from here. You lost it during our fight. Come out now with your hands up."

Birch stuck the knife back in his boot. He knew he couldn't get close enough to use it. His eye caught sight of a large, sturdy stick, possibly a branch from a Joshua tree.

He grabbed it and crouched, at the ready.

"All right, then," Jasper said, "I'm comin' in after you." As Jasper rushed around the rock, Birch took a mighty swing, catching the outlaw's knees. There was a loud crack and Jasper went down, howling in pain. The gun flew into the air, landing with a thud just a few yards away from Birch.

Birch emerged from behind the outcropping and headed toward the gun, but Jasper's hand shot out and grabbed Birch's ankle, causing him to lose his balance. As Birch struggled with Jasper, he realized that he hadn't heard any shooting for a few minutes. Jasper was on his knees, a rock in his hand, raising it above his head. Birch rolled out of the way, his hand touching cold metal. He grabbed the gun and held it on Jasper.

"Put it down slowly," he said, gasping from the exertion.

Jasper snarled and launched himself at Birch, rock at the ready. Birch pulled the trigger. The outlaw twitched once from the force of the bullet, blood seeping from a chest wound. The rock dropped from his limp hand and Jasper fell onto his side. The life drained out of his eyes, but the hate remained there.

The sound of a horse galloping away alerted Birch to the situation. He managed to stand, half crouched in case someone decided to shoot at him again. Cautiously, he made his way to the wagon. Both twins were sprawled on the ground, their weapons beside them. Both were dead — one killed by Birch's bullet, the other felled by Hogan's carbine.

Aside from the two horses attached to the wagon, three riderless horses milled around, calmly nibbling the desert grass. These horses, Birch concluded, belonged to the three dead men that now sprawled at the foot of the mesa. But Kane Dunmore was nowhere to be found. Birch noted fresh, deep hoof tracks rounding the mesa, going the opposite direction of the way Birch had come down. While his gang kept Birch and Hogan pinned down and distracted, Kane must have tried to ambush Hogan.

"Hogan," Birch called out.

There was no reply.

Birch grabbed the reins of the closest of the three horses and lifted himself into the saddle. Climbing the hill as fast as he could, Birch was afraid of what he would find — Hogan bleeding to death, Hogan already dead, having bravely defended the treasure in the ruins. What Birch saw when he reached the top of the mesa was nothing. No Hogan, no Kane, no Cactus. Even the carbine was gone. Hogan must have taken Cactus, either to escape or to follow a retreating Kane Dunmore.

Birch tracked Cactus's hoof prints through the ruins and started to descend the back side of the plateau. As he peered out across the land, the moon still high in the sky, he hoped to spot Hogan or Dunmore, but nothing moved on the shadowy landscape dotted with plateaus. Assuming Hogan had escaped and Dunmore was following, where would Hogan go from here? Birch asked himself. Why would Kane go after Hogan now, if the treasure was buried here? Of course Birch had only Hogan's word on that, and Birch had learned over the last week with Hogan, that his word was not to be trusted.

The gold didn't matter to Birch. He wanted to get Hogan, and if he caught up with Kane Dunmore as well, all the better. Besides, Hogan had his horse. Birch wanted Cactus back.

He was pulled up short by the dilemma of the wagon. Taking it with him would slow him considerably, but he couldn't just leave it.

Birch finally led the wagon and horses up the back of the mesa, leaving the bodies behind. It took a little time, but the horses would be sheltered. There was a shallow well with a little water near the center of the ruins, and enough wild grass for the horses to graze on until Birch had caught up to Hogan. He would be back for the wagon and the other horses later, or he would send someone back for them. It would depend on if he found Hogan and if the wagon was needed for the job he had intended to do with it.

Turning the unfamiliar horse he was riding in the direction the fresh hoofprints had taken, Birch spurred the animal to a gallop.

CHAPTER 19

Hiding the wagon and horses had taken precious time, and Birch spent the few remaining hours of darkness riding in the direction of the tracks. The sun had just begun to rise when he entered the outskirts of Nuevo Choix, a town nestled in a bend of the Rio Grande. As he rode along the river, he passed women who were up early to do their washing on the banks, using flat stones to lay the fabric out to dry in the full heat of the sun. Some of the women had been in the river before washing their clothes, and Birch noted the long, wet hair that hung down their backs like dark, thick ropes. A few women looked up with curious expressions as he passed by.

In the center of Nuevo Choix was a little adobe church with a big steeple and a bell that gleamed in the strong light of day. He was tempted to stop and go inside. The interior looked cool and inviting, but Birch knew that it was more likely to be hot and stuffy. If Hogan had stopped here in town, Birch mused, it was not at a church. As he rode down the main street, he spotted Cactus tethered outside a saloon called the Desert Rose. A strong wave of relief swept over Birch when he saw Cactus calmly taking water from the trough.

Birch stopped, dismounted, and tethered his horse next to Cactus. Patting Cactus's nose affectionately, he then entered the Desert Rose. It was a room about the size of Hogan's cantina in Canutillo. Birch was parched from breathing in the desert dust. He ordered a whiskey and looked around. Hogan was nowhere to be found. There were no back doors or upstairs rooms to check in the Desert Rose. He came to the conclusion that Hogan had left Cactus outside the saloon as a decoy, but Birch was confident that Hogan wasn't far from here.

Birch's thoughts turned to Kane Dunmore. He hadn't really noticed the kind of horse Dunmore was riding. Not knowing Dunmore's whereabouts worried Birch more than Hogan's whereabouts.

Birch turned to the bartender. "Has an older fellow come in here recently, white hair, mole on his nose, gaunt?"

The bartender, a large, balding man with

a squint, eyed Birch with misgiving. He grunted in the negative and turned away to serve another customer. A moment later, a woman was at his side, an empty glass in her hand. She was heavily made up with rouge and powder, her dull brown hair was pushed up on top of her head, and she was dressed in a gaudy, revealing yellow dress that advertised her charms.

She leaned toward Birch, all the better to show herself off to advantage, and held up her glass. "For the price of a drink," she said in a sultry voice that didn't fit with the rest of her, "I can tell you where to find him, stranger."

Birch gave her a hard look. His distrust must have shown through, because she added, "I saw him come in here less than an hour ago, and it was me who sent him on to the place he was asking about."

An alarm went off in Birch's head. Remembering the man's cry back at the pueblo ruins, he wondered if Hogan had sought medical help. "You sent him to a doctor?"

She laughed and held up her glass. "He didn't look that bad off. Just like he'd been out in the desert too long. I sent him over to Mae's place."

Birch didn't have to ask what kind of "place" Mae's was. It was most likely a cathouse. He ordered a drink for the girl, then turned and asked, "Has any other stranger been in here recently, a dark, husky man with a black beard?"

She tossed her glass of rye down like it was water, then wiped her mouth before answering. "No," she said, shaking her head. "Haven't seen anyone like that around here. I don't suppose you'd buy me another?" She batted her eyelashes at him and pressed her body against Birch. Her lilac water filled his nostrils, and it was not unappealing. Her bloodshot, watery eyes were half closed, and her rouged lips smiled at him uncertainly. His only feeling was of wanting to find Hogan as fast as possible. Birch placed another coin on the counter for her, smiled, and started to leave, hearing the joy in her voice as she thanked him.

Outside, Birch got on Cactus and, taking the reins of the other horse, then started asking for directions to Mae's. Like most cathouses, Mae's was on the edge of town and easy enough to find. Since Nuevo Choix was small, Mae's wasn't far from the saloon. Even a sickly old man like Hogan could walk there in five minutes if he was so inclined. And Hogan must have been inclined, to leave a trail as obvious as this one. When he left Birch at the ruins, Hogan must have known that he was going to be caught.

Mae's was a large adobe building like all the others. The one difference was that the door was an ornately carved piece of exotic dark wood, no doubt from a wealthy admirer and frequent customer. Cherubs leered out of the corners of the door, while a violent arrangement of flowers and leaves fought for the center of it. Birch was reluctant to knock for fear of grazing his knuckles on one of the sharp reliefs.

A pudgy woman about forty years old answered the door, wearing a thin white muslin robe with a plunging neckline that displayed her ample bosom. She could have been the saloon girl's older sister, or maybe her mother. She wore her brassy gold hair in a messy arrangement on top of her head, a variety of tortoiseshell and mother-of-pearl combs stuck in wherever she could find a place. The woman looked coyly at Birch before letting him inside.

"Come in, stranger. Make yourself at home," she said in a throaty voice. "What can I get for you today?" She brushed up against him in the small vestibule and ushered him into the parlor. Three women were lounging on overstuffed furniture, all in various stages of undress. One young girl wore a long-skirt chemise and lace-trimmed drawers underneath. An older woman, somewhere in her late twenties, wore a moth-eaten pink silk dressing gown over a plain cotton underskirt, and little more. The third woman, who was a tired-looking twenty-two or twenty-three years old, wore a camisole and drawers.

When Birch entered, they all perked up, trying to look as comely as possible. Birch had the feeling that the women came to attention not because of him, but because of the madam's subtle gestures behind his back.

He turned back to the madam and said, "Actually, I came here on business."

She fluttered up to him, a knowing look in her eye, and laid a hand on his arm. "Well, of course you did. All our gentlemen callers come here on business. Mae is always discreet." Birch understood from the way that she talked that she was Mae and was talking about herself in the third person.

The three women, Birch noticed out of the corner of his eye, had gone back to looking tired and hopeless. The oldest of the three was fanning herself with a limp homemade fan. The other two were quietly fighting over a pair of lace gloves that had been lying on the parlor table when he came in.

"No, you don't understand," Birch said firmly. "I'm looking for a man."

The three women stopped what they were doing. Mae's eyes widened for a moment, and Birch hurriedly continued, "He came here less than an hour ago."

Mae drew herself up with as much dignity as she could muster, considering the way she was dressed, and slowly replied, "I don't think we can help you here." She turned sharply to the girls and said, "Why don't you girls go out to the kitchen and make some coffee."

The three women stopped what they were doing, got up, and obediently filed out of the parlor. Meanwhile, Mae got a firm grip on Birch's arm, obviously with the intention of escorting him out the door before he made any trouble. Her other hand was stuck in a pocket of her gown, a discreet bulge announcing that she carried a derringer. Before she could act, there was a loud whoop that brought Birch up short. It seemed to come from a room down a corridor off the parlor.

Birch broke away from the madam and started down the corridor. "You can't go down there without my permission," Mae called after him, distress in her voice.

Only one door was closed. When Birch opened it, he was almost sorry he had. There was Hogan in his undershirt and pants with suspenders, reclining on a lumpy bed, a woman on either side. Both women were dressed in the same manner as the ones in the parlor. Birch's eyes widened.

"Well, hello, son. Glad you got here so soon," Hogan said, grinning ear to ear. "This here is Maude," he nodded to a lanky, pale redhead on his right, "and this one's Esther." Esther was a ruddy brunet who looked as if she had spent her entire young life milking cows. She studied Birch with interest. Maude giggled.

Under different circumstances, Birch might have found the scene amusing. Mae stood right behind him, puffing from the effort to keep up with him. "I tried to stop him, Tom, but he's too bullheaded," she said with obvious affection for Hogan.

Hogan removed his arm from behind the reclining Maude and waved away Mae's distress. "That's fine. This here's my son."

Mae squeezed past Birch to get a better look at him. She studied him as if she had to memorize his features. Finally, she brightened. "Oh, I see it now. Yes, he has your eyes, Tom. And your chin and nose."

Birch narrowed his eyes. Hogan seemed to sense that things were not going well and shooed the girls away. "I think my son wants to talk to me privately, Mae. Thanks for the company."

Mae hurried her girls out of the room, all three women giving Birch a curious, interested glance as they passed by him. When Birch shut the door, Hogan was putting on his shirt and boots.

"Why did you leave me back there?" Birch asked quietly.

Hogan shrugged. "I was scared. I used up all the carbine shells and Kane Dunmore realized it. He started climbing the mesa with a gun in his hand. And you can bet it wasn't empty. So I jumped on Cactus and headed out of there like hell was on my heels." He looked up pointedly at Birch and added, "And it might well have been."

"Didn't Kane follow you?" Birch asked, puzzled. He knew he hadn't passed Dunmore, and he hadn't seen any sign of him in Nuevo Choix so far. He had already decided that Hogan hadn't been telling the truth and that the buried gold was not in the mesa ruins. Hogan should, by all accounts, be in Kane's custody right now and they should be heading for the real place where the gold was buried. Birch felt uneasy. Hogan hadn't exactly been stealthy in his flight. He had left tracks that a child could follow.

"Hogan," Birch said, calmer this time, "is

the gold buried back there or was that just another story you told?"

Hogan looked down, then back up at Birch, his eyes gleaming. "That's really where the gold is buried. I'm not lying to you, Jefferson. And I didn't lie to Kane. But he won't believe that until he sees the gold with his own eyes. Maybe that's where he is right now." Then he had a coughing spell.

Birch turned it around in his mind. That would explain why Kane Dunmore hadn't gone after Hogan. During the gunfight, Dunmore must have realized that the rest of his gang had been killed or captured. He must have seen or heard Tom Hogan leaving, and instead of chasing him, he took a chance that the gold was buried where Hogan said it was. So he hid out until Birch left, going after his escaped prisoner, even going so far as to hide his horse to create the deception that he had gone after Hogan. He was a mean son of a bitch who would undoubtedly hunt Hogan down for what he'd done, but first he would get the gold.

Birch leaned over and absently patted Hogan's back until he stopped coughing. "Hogan, are you willing to return the gold for a lighter prison sentence?"

The older man turned around until Birch could see the resignation in his eyes. "I guess so." He shrugged.

Birch frowned. "You don't sound real certain."

Hogan sighed heavily. "Jefferson, you don't leave me much choice. If I go in with you, but without the gold, I'll never get out of prison alive. If I go in with the gold, there's a chance I'll still be alive when they let me out. But the consumption will most likely take me either way."

Birch avoided Hogan's steady gaze. "Well, then," he said gruffly, "let's go get that gold, and maybe find Kane Dunmore as well."

CHAPTER 20

The sun was past high noon, but their shadows lagged behind them as Birch and Hogan urged their horses on at a breakneck gallop. If they could keep up the pace, Birch figured they would get to the pueblo ruins before Kane Dunmore dug up all the gold and left.

Birch slowed Cactus about a quarter of a mile away from the ruins, Hogan following his lead. They slid off their horses and walked the rest of the way, coming up the back side of the mesa.

"If Kane's still there, he can hear almost everything from up there," Hogan pointed out. "That's why it was such a good idea when I chose that spot. I had no idea that it would backfire on me."

"Why don't you stay here with the horses and I'll go up there first," Birch suggested, drawing his gun.

Hogan grumbled a bit but let Birch go ahead.

Birch climbed the steep path carved into the mesa, keeping his head down in case there was any shooting. When he was near the crest, he froze and listened, but heard no sound from inside the ruins. Finally, he straightened up slightly for a better look.

He scanned the ruins, but there was no sign that anyone had been up there recently. Cautiously, Birch looked around, still certain that at any moment Kane Dunmore would appear. Birch made his way through the mazelike ruins and peered down. He could see Hogan standing with the horses, shifting from one foot to the other.

"It took you long enough," Hogan called up to Birch. "Can I come up now?"

Birch waved to Hogan, who led Cactus and his horse up the mesa. It took him some time, but he waved aside Birch's offer of help. When he got to the top, he was wheezing. Birch unloaded the shovels and told Hogan to tether the horses.

"Where do we start?" Birch asked. Despite the circumstances, he felt a growing excitement at digging for treasure. He tried to keep his emotions in control, because he needed to stay sharp and alert.

Still slightly breathless from the exertion, Hogan was half bent over, his hands on his knees. He lifted one hand and pointed toward the middle of the ruins, to the deep circular pit that Birch had noticed during the gunfight with the Dunmores. It probably had been a central meeting house when the ruins were a thriving pueblo village.

"I buried it near the wall in the southwest corner," Hogan explained. "Lewis marked it for me."

Birch looked at the structure and frowned. There was no corner. Had Hogan's wits been addled by the climb?

Hogan must have noticed Birch's puzzled look. "Hold on. I can tell you exactly where it was buried." He climbed down into the pit, looked at the position of the sun, and located the southwest area. Then he bent over the low stone wall, ravaged by time, climate, and maybe a battle that took place long ago, and pointed to a faint X that was marked on one of the stones. Hogan positioned himself in front of the marker, turned around and took five paces toward the middle, then stopped. "Right here."

Birch dug first, allowing Hogan to rest from his climb. The earth was packed down and hard going, but as the hole got deeper, the digging became easier. He worked for about thirty minutes in silence, then stopped to take some water from his saddle canteen. Although it was a couple of hours from dusk, the temperature had dropped. Still, Birch's shirt was stuck to his back.

Hogan chuckled, resting against the ruins. "Watching you work reminds me of the time you wanted to plant a little vegetable garden when we lived in Canutillo."

Birch rested against his shovel, taking another swig of tepid water. "I remember that. We had a pretty good garden that year."

Hogan dropped his gaze. "Actually, your mother and I had to replant the seeds for you. They were too close together. Got up two hours earlier than usual to do it before I left for my Tucson mail run."

Birch put the shovel down and took off his shirt. He didn't want to work long with his shirt off; he burned easily. But he wanted his shirt to dry. With another cautious look around, Birch also took his gun belt off. It was a shallow hole now, and Hogan had told him that the hole for the gold had been four feet deep. He estimated that he had another half hour of work ahead of him.

"Why don't you let me take a stab at it," Hogan said, getting up.

"Sure you feel well enough to dig?" Birch asked, dropping his shovel gratefully.

"Why don't you both dig?" a third voice asked.

Birch slowly turned around.

Kane Dunmore's eyes burned with hate. "Fooled you all, didn't I?" Dunmore chuckled. "I even hid my horse so you thought I was gone," Dunmore said to them. Birch thought he recognized a gleam of madness in the outlaw's face as he turned to look at the ex–Texas Ranger. "You were the one who killed my brother and cousins." Dunmore's bushy black eyebrows furrowed together in a look of disapproval.

Birch kept his hands where Dunmore could see them and made no sudden moves. "I'm sorry about your family," he said slowly. Out of the corner of his eye, Birch saw Hogan swallow, beads of sweat running down his forehead. Birch focused back on Dunmore and repeated, "I'm sorry I had to kill your brother and cousins, but I was just defending myself and Hogan."

Suddenly, Dunmore broke out into a smile. "This way," he said with a shrug, "there's more gold for me." With his gun, he gestured to the shovels by Hogan and Birch's feet. "Now you just pick those up and start digging. You'd better find that treasure and load it up for me, if you want me to let you live."

Birch wasn't counting on Dunmore's being a man of his word, but he picked up his shovel, as did Hogan. They began to make short work of the next few feet. When Hogan's shovel struck something with a dull thud, Birch knew his father hadn't been lying.

As they brushed aside the last layer of dirt, Birch glanced at an increasingly excited Kane Dunmore, whose gun hand was shaking. Birch had seen plenty of gold fever in the mining camps he'd worked in or traveled through.

Birch furtively tried to locate where he'd let his gun belt fall. He was still silently admonishing himself for letting his guard down like that. But he had to admit that it had been difficult to work with a gun strapped to his thigh. Even if he had been wearing his gun, he wouldn't have been able to draw fast enough when Dunmore showed himself.

Dunmore wasn't so deranged that he hadn't noticed Birch's search for his gun. "Get back to work," he ordered Birch in a high voice. "You won't reach your gun in time."

Hogan started coughing suddenly and Dunmore pivoted in Hogan's direction, his gun wavering between his two prisoners. Birch took a chance with the distraction and swung his spade. Dunmore noticed, aimed, and shot at Birch. There was a loud clang, then Birch felt a tingling sensation up his arms. At the same time, Hogan was doubled over, moaning.

A confused Dunmore stared at Birch, then looked over at Hogan.

Without hesitation, Birch slammed the shovel's blade against Dunmore's head. For a moment the outlaw stood perfectly still, as if he hadn't felt a thing. Then Dunmore fell to his knees, the gun dropping from his limp hand. He hit the ground facedown.

Birch turned his attention to Hogan, who stood clutching his side. Blood seeped out from a hole torn in his dust-covered shirt just under his ribs. Hogan let out a sigh of exasperation.

"Damn!" he said weakly. "That shovel of yours saved you. The bullet must've ricocheted off it and hit me."

Birch looked silently at the metal blade, noting the large dent where the bullet had rebounded. He dropped the shovel on the ground and went over to Hogan. Taking the canteen from Cactus's saddle and a handkerchief from one of the saddlebags, Birch cleaned up the area around Hogan's wound as best he could, all the while maintaining silence as Hogan swore up a blue streak.

"What're you doin'?" Hogan asked indignantly. He flinched as Birch's fingers explored the wound.

"Searching for the bullet."

Hogan turned cantankerous. "I know it's in there, damn it. You don't have to go stickin' your finger where it has no business bein'." He moved away from Birch, who straightened up.

Birch noticed an exit hole when Hogan turned away from him. He was relieved that the bullet hadn't lodged in Hogan's rib cage. "I think you'll live."

"No thanks to you," Hogan snapped. "Now what're we goin' to do with this fellow?"

They turned their attention to Kane Dunmore. Birch reached down and picked up Kane's gun, then retrieved his own gun belt.

"Jefferson," Hogan called. He was bent over Dunmore. "I don't think this one's alive." He straightened, wincing a bit.

Birch came back and examined the outlaw leader. Then he glanced back at his ashen-faced father. "Maybe you better sit in the wagon. I'll do the work," Birch said.

Hogan didn't have the strength to disagree with him. By the time Birch got Hogan in the front seat, his father had passed out.

CHAPTER 21

Winslow came around from behind his desk to shake Birch's hand. Tisdale stood off to the side. Birch observed with amusement that his employer's face was red and his nose was peeling after a week in Albuquerque. He was no longer wearing a black woolen suit; it had been replaced by light-colored lightweight trousers, a stiffly starched white cotton shirt with a string tie, and a vest. He held a wide-brimmed hat in his hands.

"I just want to tell you how pleased I am that you brought back the gold," Winslow said, pumping Birch's hand genially, a relieved expression on his face. "I must confess that I was worried about you when we received word that you had been sidetracked a few days ago."

Worried about the gold more likely, Birch thought. He looked over at Tisdale, who seemed equally relieved. Birch was sure

Tisdale had been nervous after receiving Birch's last wire a few days ago, telling his employer only what was necessary — that Birch would not arrive in Albuquerque as scheduled, but would be coming back soon and would wire again if there were any complications.

Tisdale spoke up. "I was surprised to receive a wire from the Raton marshal that the Dunmore gang is dead. How did you manage to track them down?"

Birch suppressed a smile. "It wasn't a matter of me finding them. They found me. And Tom Hogan."

Winslow wore the frown of a businessman who has had to compromise. But there was no doubt that he had come out ahead in the bargain. "Yes. We were talking earlier, Mr. Tisdale and I, and we wondered why you didn't bring Hogan in as well. I can only assume that he escaped."

"Yes, he did," Birch said in a noncommittal tone.

"A substantial reward will be offered by the Santa Fe railroad if you would like to go after him again," Winslow said.

Birch avoided the vice president's eyes for a moment, then looked straight at him. "I don't think you have to worry about Tom Hogan robbing any more trains," he replied.

"I was told that after he escaped, he died of consumption. I wasn't able to go after the body. He was already buried somewhere in Texas."

Winslow's eyes looked beyond Birch's right shoulder to Tisdale, then back to Birch. He nodded. "All right. I guess I'll have to take your word for it. But I won't be able to pay you double the reward without Tom Hogan's body here."

Birch shrugged. "If my sources are wrong, and Hogan causes any further trouble for you, I'll come back and track him down. No cost." He could feel Tisdale's eyes boring into his back, furious that the agency had lost the bonus on Hogan and that Birch would offer his services for free. But he couldn't be too upset, since he was getting a nice bonus for the Dunmore gang and the returned gold.

They left the railroad office, silent until they were outside.

"All right, Birch," Tisdale said. "I'm willing to bet that wasn't the real story back there. Hogan's alive, isn't he? I know you well enough to know there's more to all this!"

Birch didn't reply immediately. Instead he steered Tisdale into a nearby cantina for tequila and a meal. As they sat at a small

213

clean table, the air was filled with the spicy aroma of Mexican cooking.

"Look, Birch," an astonished Tisdale began, "I know that whatever you did was for a good reason. But I am your employer, and I have to be concerned about how this incident will reflect on my agency's reputation, especially if Hogan turns up again."

"It's probably best that you don't know what really happened. As far as I'm concerned," Birch said, "Tom Hogan is dead and will remain so. I will take the responsibility if he shows up again."

Tisdale ordered a plate of tamales, rice, and pulque. "I've taken a liking to the drink," he explained to Birch. "It has a pleasant aroma and a sweet taste." A tumbler filled with pulque was placed in front of him. "Maybe I can bring a jug of it home with me," he added wistfully, forgetting that he had been frustrated with Birch a moment ago as he tasted the nectar.

Birch quietly sipped his tequila.

CHAPTER 22

His employer, full of pulque, spent an hour singing tasteless songs in the cantina until Birch paid the bill and helped Tisdale back to his hotel. He even packed Tisdale's bags and took him to the train, waiting until the train pulled away. He would always remember watching Tisdale wave a jug of pulque out the window as the train left the station.

He had asked the conductor, not Ned Murchison this time, to look after Tisdale until he had slept off the effects. One good thing had come from Tisdale's drunk. He had given Birch his pay right on the spot, adding a generous bonus for delivering much more than had been expected.

Birch loaded up his own gear and rode Cactus out of Albuquerque. He headed for the little town of Nuevo Choix.

In Nuevo Choix, Birch came to the house on the edge of town. Mae didn't answer the door this time. Maude, the pale redhead, fluttered her eyelashes at him.

"How's he doing?" Birch asked as she let him inside.

"He's been running Mae ragged," Maude said, rolling her eyes. She led him into the parlor and they sat on the settee. "Would you like a drink?" she asked.

Hat in hand, Birch accepted.

From down the hall, a familiar voice bellowed. "Mae! I need more whiskey for the pain. Leave the bottle this time."

"Keep your voice down, Tom," Mae called back from another room. Birch could hear the impatience in her voice as she bustled down the hall and opened a door. "There are working girls here," she scolded. "I don't want our customers to get the idea that we run a hospital."

A few minutes later, Mae entered the parlor where Maude was sitting with Birch. When she saw Birch, her mouth turned down slightly. "I expected to see you yesterday. That father of yours has been a handful. All he wants is either whiskey or pulque. Getting him to eat is as hard as stacking hay one straw at a time."

Hogan shuffled into the room, leaning on a cane. "Eating your food requires gallons of pulque to wash it down with," he replied. Mae turned and made a face at him.

Amused but anxious to be on his way, Birch stood and pulled some paper money and coins from his pocket and gave it to Mae. "This is for your trouble."

She took it and counted, her face softening. "Why, thank you, Mr. Birch." Mae was practically beaming as she fingered the notes. "Tom here is welcome anytime. As long as you pay me as much as you did today." She patted Hogan on the back. He snarled in return.

Birch turned to Hogan. "So has the doctor given you permission to be up and walking?"

"I'm fine," Hogan said gruffly. "I suppose it's time to go to Albuquerque and face my accusers." Coughing slightly, he walked stiffly, and with the support of his cane, to the door.

"You're dead now," Birch said.

Hogan froze, then turned around. "What? You're going to kill me? I know I wasn't much of a father to you, but — "

Birch allowed himself to smile a little, and he shook his head. "No, I mean, I told them back in Albuquerque that you died after you escaped from me. Said you were buried somewhere in Texas."

"Why, Jefferson. That was mighty nice of you. Thank you." He seemed on the verge of adding "son," but restrained himself.

"But," Birch replied sharply, "no more train robberies. Your days as an outlaw are finished. If I ever hear that you've taken it up again, I'll come after you and kill you myself. I mean it."

Hogan's eyes misted slightly. "Why did you do this, son? Why do a favor for a father you'd rather forget?"

Birch looked away. "I can't say I approve of your calling. But you are blood kin, and I can't ignore that." He looked back at Hogan and added, "Go back to Canutillo and marry Maria. Help her run the cantina."

"Will you ever come visit me?" Hogan asked, moving a little closer to Birch, who had stiffened.

After a moment of silence, Birch shook his head. "I don't think so. Our time has passed. Just look out for Lupe and her mother. And keep Lewis out of trouble."

Hogan and Birch walked outside, and Birch got back in the saddle.

"Jefferson, there's so much I want to know about you. There's so much time we could make up for."

Birch was aware of the pleading in Hogan's voice, but he knew it was too late for them. There was too much pain in their past. And there was so little time left for Tom Hogan.

His father would be better off spending it with the people who had taken him in as family so many years ago.

"Go back to Canutillo, Hogan," Birch said again. "Go home."

When Birch looked down into his father's face he noticed the old man appeared more resigned, almost at peace with the past. As Birch turned Cactus around and headed out of town, he thought about following his own advice. He couldn't live in the past either, back before his beloved wife and son died, but he wasn't going to spend the rest of his life running from his memories.

The employees of THORNDIKE PRESS hope you have enjoyed this Large Print book. All our Large Print books are designed for easy reading — and they're made to last.

Other Thorndike Large Print books are available at your library, through selected bookstores, or directly from us. Suggestions for books you would like to see in Large Print are always welcome.

For more information about current and upcoming titles, please call or mail your name and address to:

THORNDIKE PRESS
PO Box 159
Thorndike, Maine 04986
800/223-6121
207/948-2962